Read all the Diary of a Pug books!

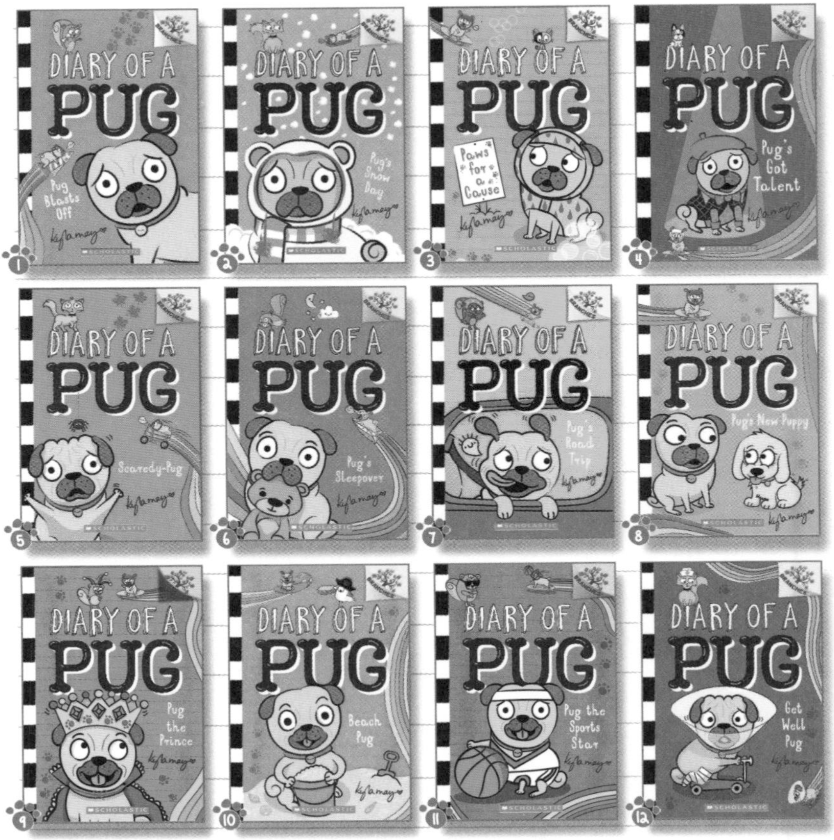
DIARY OF A PUG
Pug Blasts Off
Pug's Snow Day
Paws for a Cause
Pug's Got Talent
Scaredy-Pug
Pug's Sleepover
Pug's Road Trip
Pug's New Puppy
Pug the Prince
Beach Pug
Pug the Sports Star
Get Well Pug
SCHOLASTIC

More books coming soon!

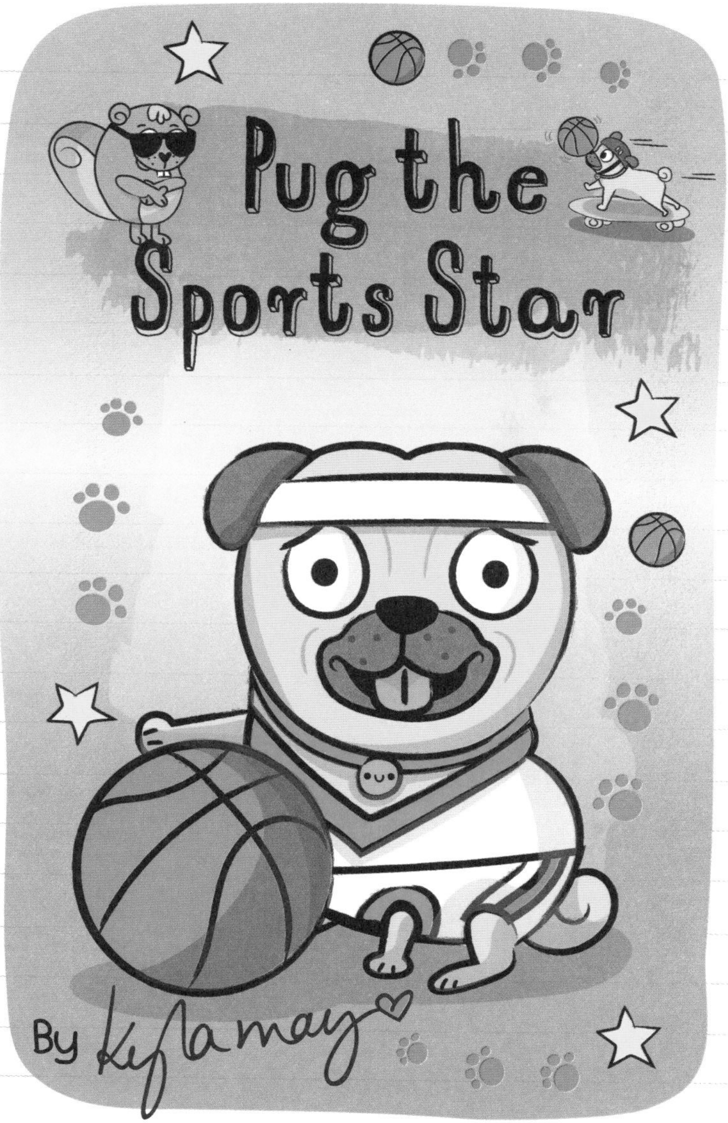
Pug the Sports Star
By Kyla May

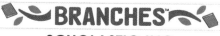

BRANCHES™
SCHOLASTIC INC.

I dedicate this book to Mikka, who I love and am so proud of. xo

Special thanks to Meredith Rusu

Art copyright © 2024 by Kyla May
Text copyright © 2024 by Scholastic Inc.

Photos © KylaMay2019

Library of Congress Cataloging-in-Publication Data
Names: May, Kyla, author, illustrator.
Title: Pug the sports star / by Kyla May.
Description: First edition. | New York: Branches/Scholastic Inc., 2024.
Series: Diary of a pug; book 11 Summary: Bub is a star with a basketball and a pug level hoop—but now Bella wants him to teach the other dogs the same trick, and Bub is not sure he wants to be in the spotlight. Identifiers: LCCN 2023034899 (print) | ISBN 9781338877632 (paperback) | 9781338877649 (library binding) | Subjects: LCSH: Pug—Juvenile fiction. | Human-animal relationships—Juvenile fiction. | Basketball stories. | Diaries—Juvenile fiction. | CYAC: Pug—Fiction. | Dogs—Fiction. | Basketball—Fiction. | Human-animal relationships—Fiction. |Diaries—Fiction. | Humorous stories. | LCGFT: Humorous fiction. | Diary fiction. Classification: LCC PZ7.M4535 Pvg 2024 (print) | DDC 813.6 [Fic—dc23/eng/20230801
LC record available at https://lccn.loc.gov/2023034899

978-1-338-87764-9 (reinforced library binding) / 978-1-338-87763-2 (paperback)

10 9 8 7 6 5 4 3 2 1   24 25 26 27 28

Printed in China 62
First edition, September 2024
Edited by AnnMarie Anderson
Book design by Kyla May and Christian Zelaya

Table of Contents

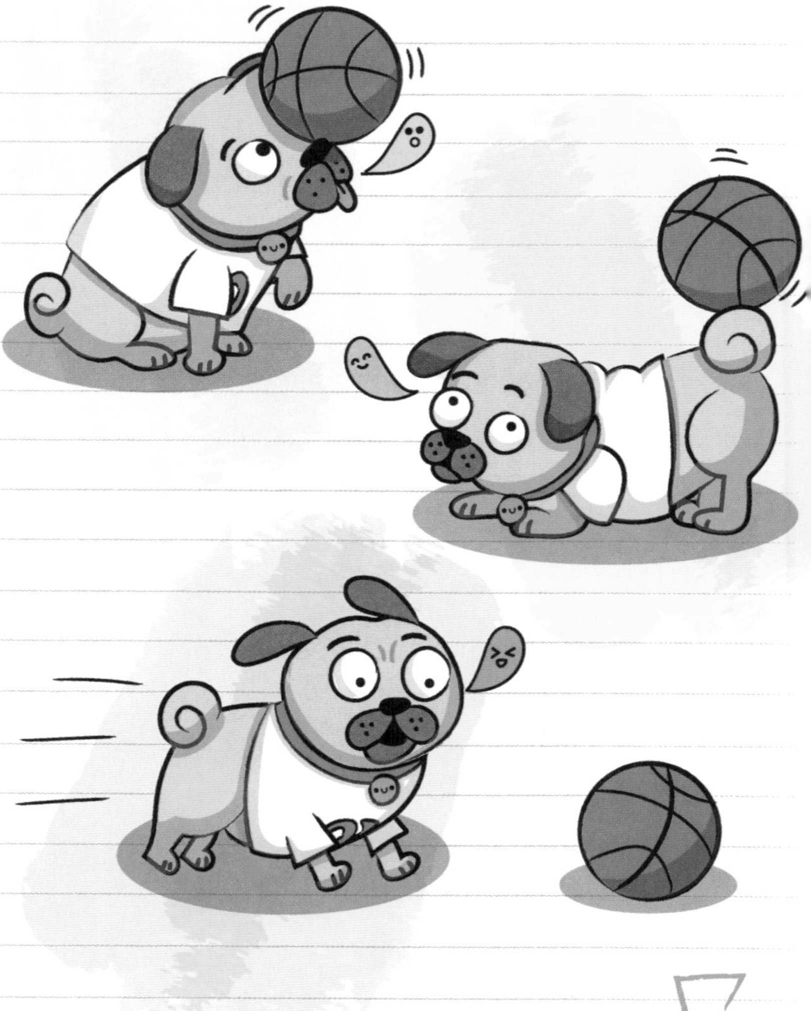

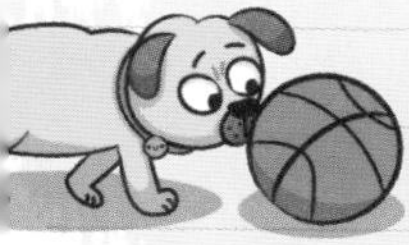

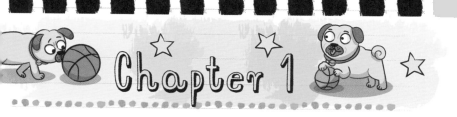

Chapter 1

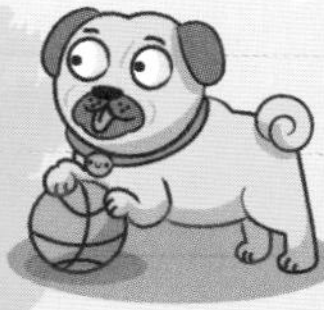

SHOOTING SOME HOOPS

MONDAY

Dear Diary,

Today I learned that I'm good at basketball. So good, I might be a sports star!

You're not going to believe how it happened. But first, here are some things to know about me.

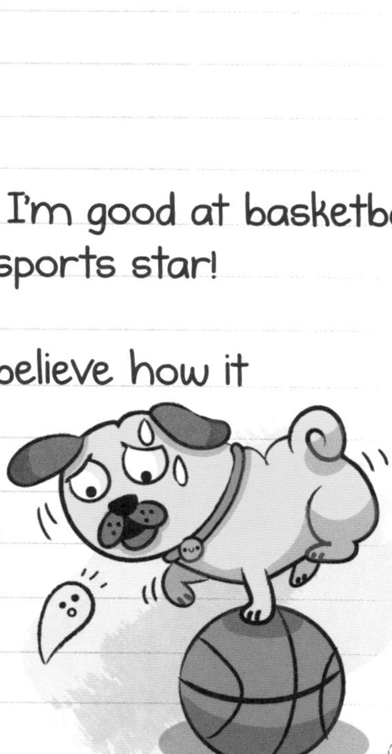

I'm a dog who can learn new tricks.

I make many different faces:

Shoe-Sniffing Face

I'm Sweaty Face

Oops Face

These are some of my favorite things:

PLAYING WITH BELLA

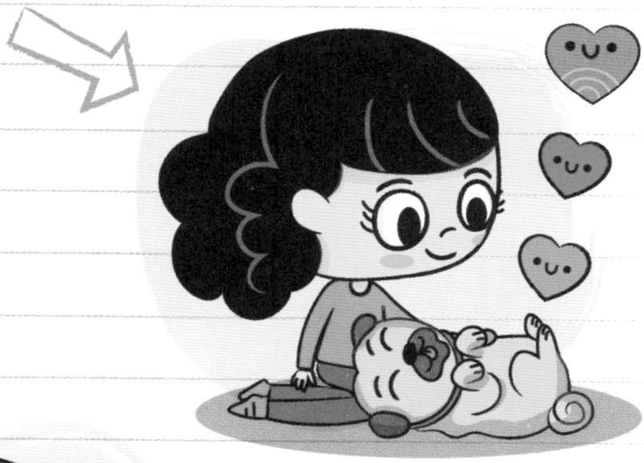

BEAR

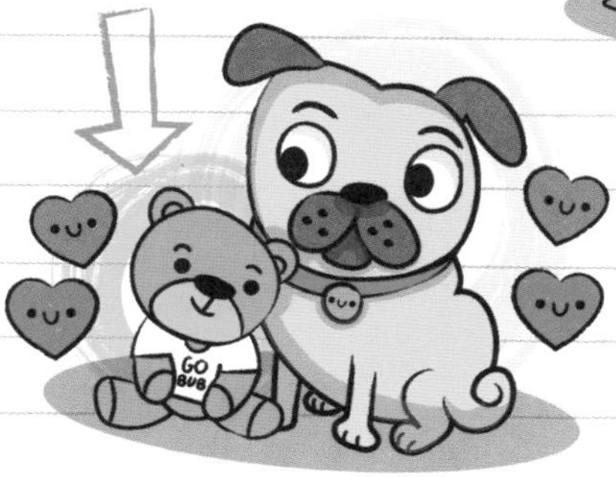
GO BUB

PEANUT BUTTER TREATS

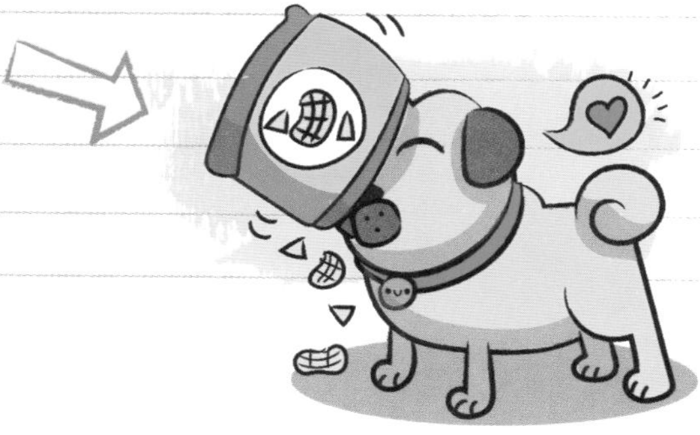

Here are some things that get on my nerves:

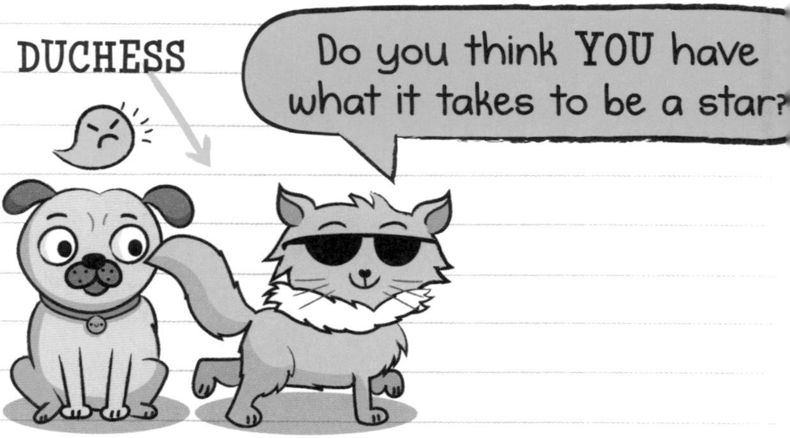
DUCHESS
Do you think YOU have what it takes to be a star?

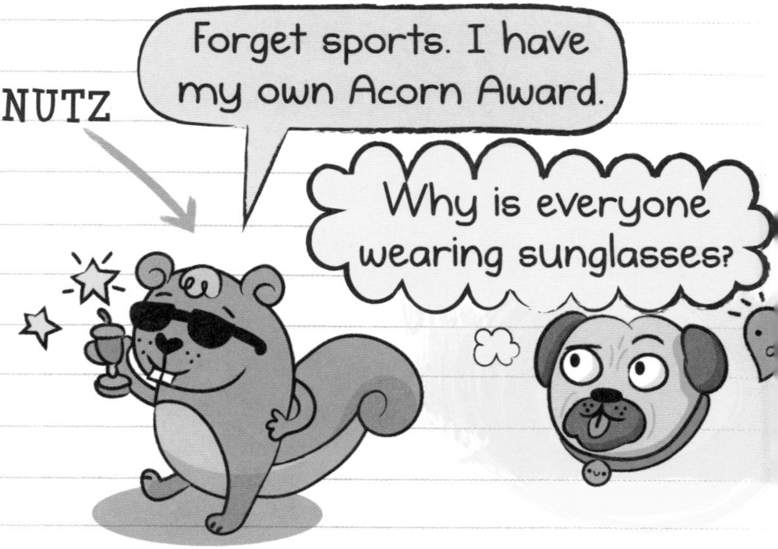
NUTZ
Forget sports. I have my own Acorn Award.
Why is everyone wearing sunglasses?

And **WATER**. I can't stand water.

It's funny because that's how I got my full name. Once, Bella was taking a bubble bath. I jumped in, too. No one told me there was water UNDER the bubbles! Bella named me **BARON VON BUBBLES** after that.

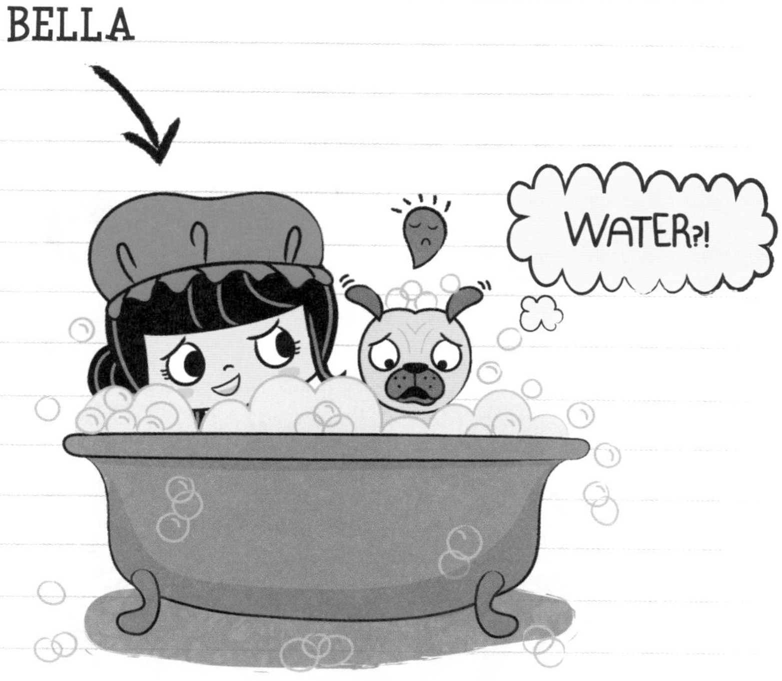
BELLA
WATER?!

But back to my story about sports stardom . . .

Bella had something to show her friend Jack after school.

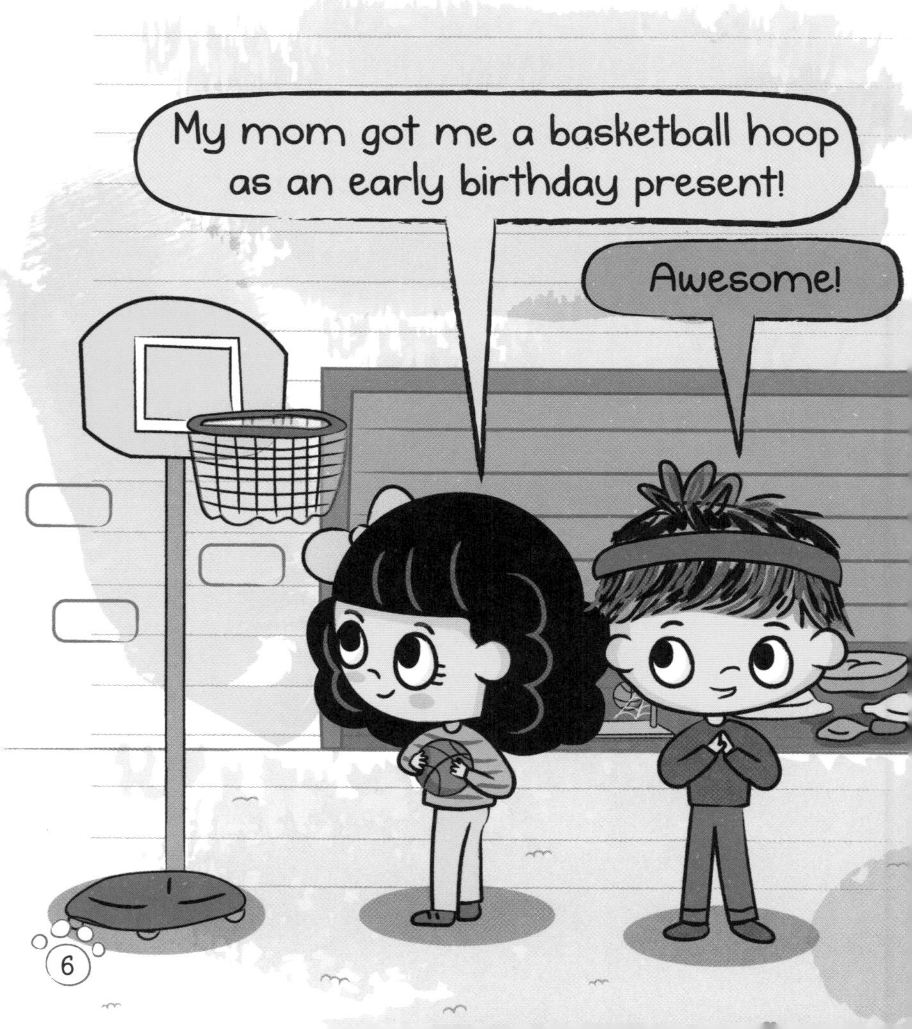
My mom got me a basketball hoop as an early birthday present!
Awesome!

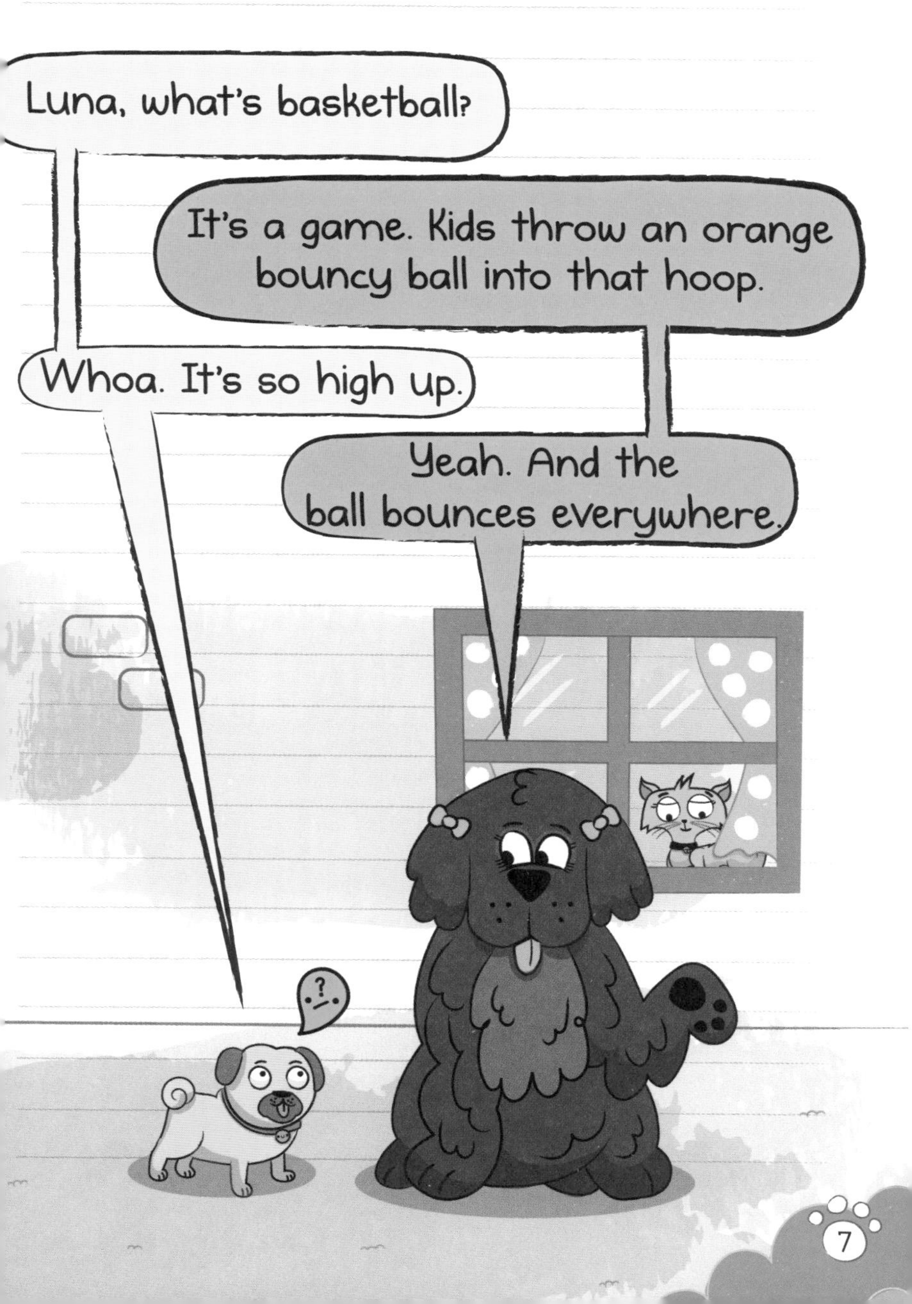
Luna, what's basketball?
It's a game. Kids throw an orange bouncy ball into that hoop.
Whoa. It's so high up.
Yeah. And the ball bounces everywhere.
?

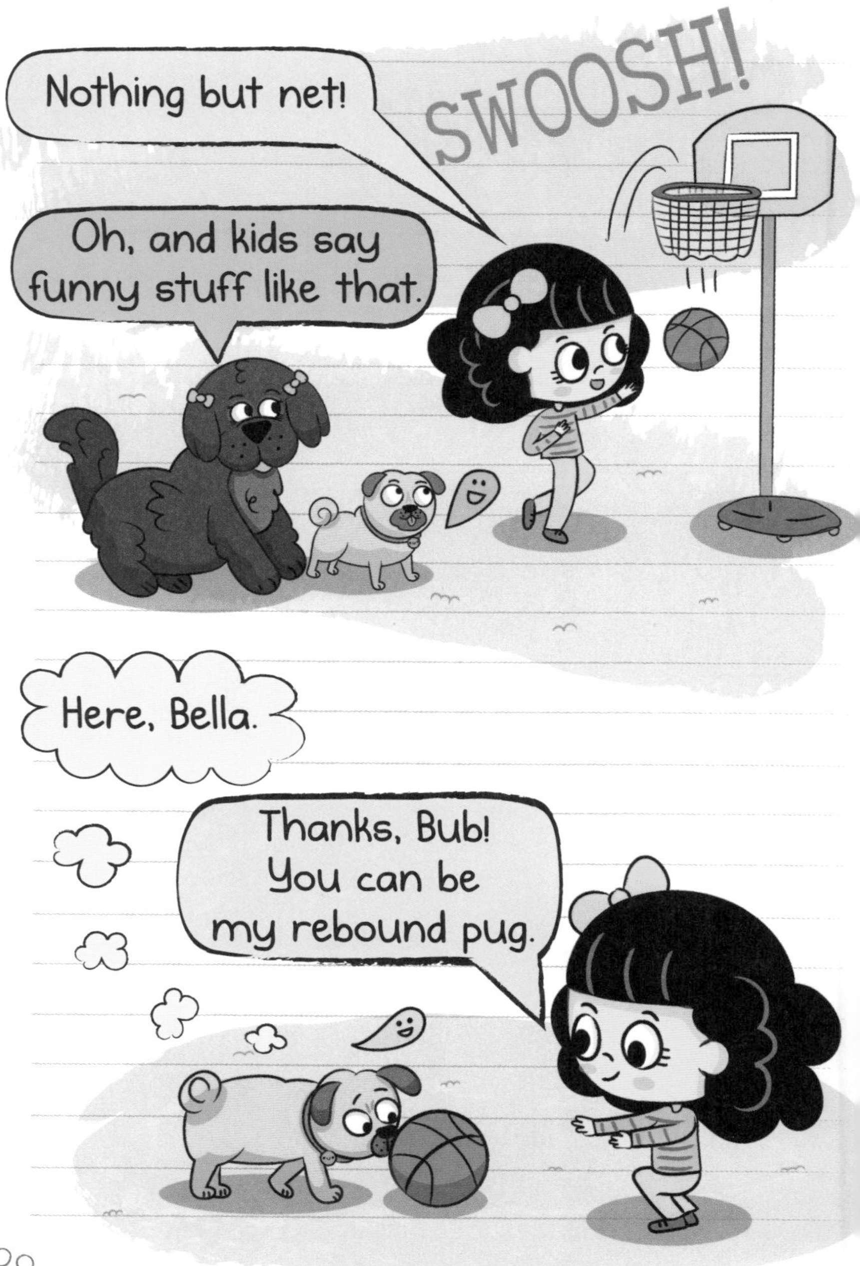
Nothing but net!
SWOOSH!
Oh, and kids say funny stuff like that.
Here, Bella.
Thanks, Bub! You can be my rebound pug.

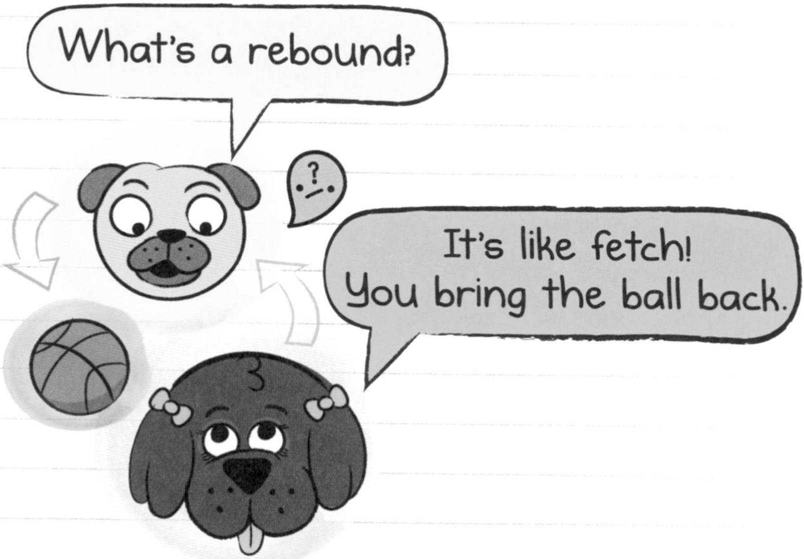
What's a rebound?
?
It's like fetch!
You bring the ball back.

Luna was right. Bella and Jack said funny words while the ball bounced EVERYWHERE.

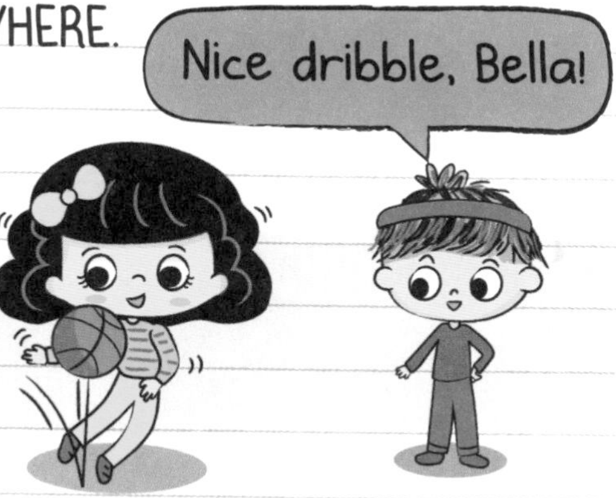
Nice dribble, Bella!

I didn't know what anything meant. But it looked fun.

And I liked chasing the ball!

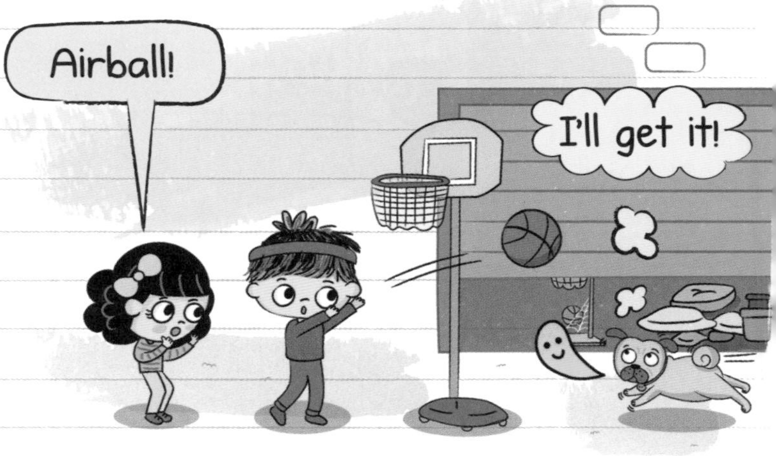
Airball!
I'll get it!

Diary, I followed the ball into the garage.

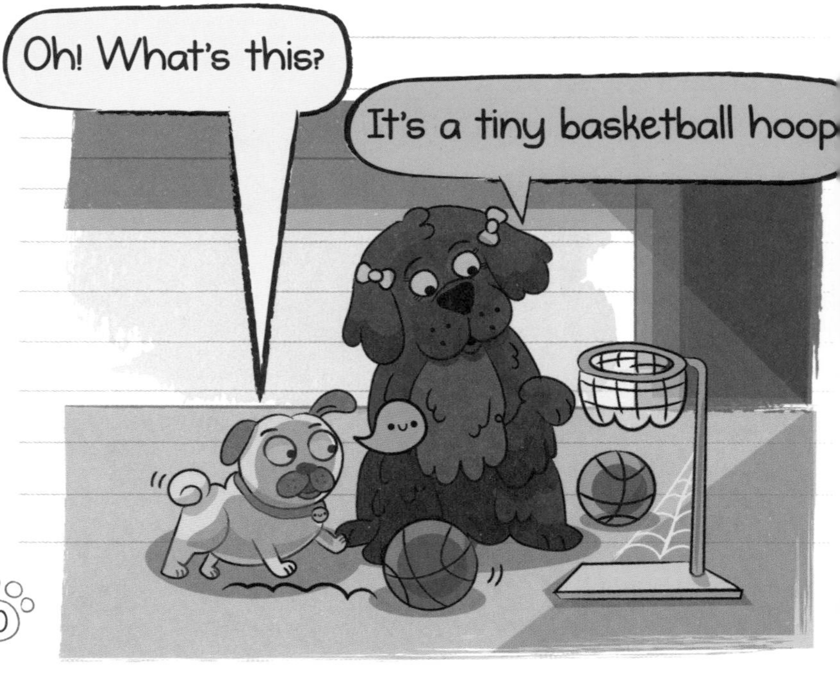
Oh! What's this?
It's a tiny basketball hoop

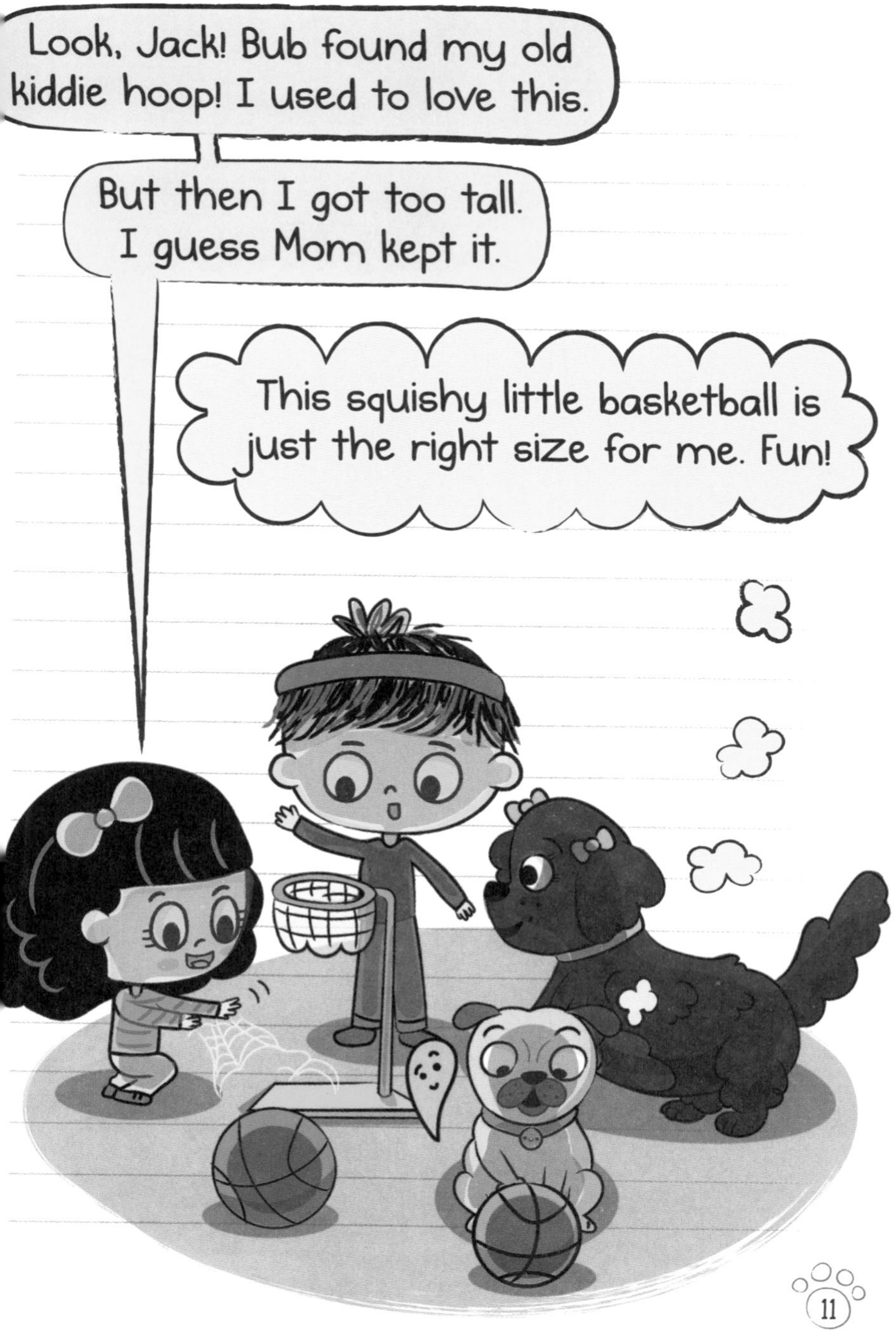
Look, Jack! Bub found my old kiddie hoop! I used to love this.
But then I got too tall. I guess Mom kept it.
This squishy little basketball is just the right size for me. Fun!

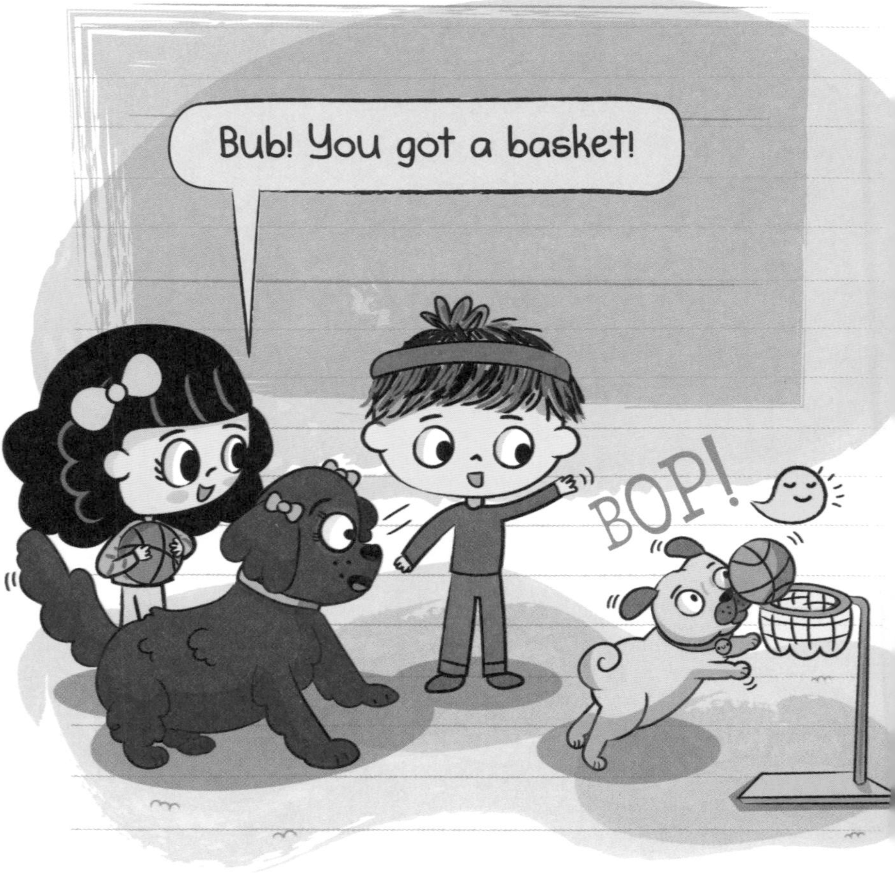
Bub! You got a basket!
BOP!

Basketball was easy, Diary! I used my nose to "scoop and bop" the ball into the hoop over and over again. (That's called making baskets.) Then something unexpected happened . . .

People walking by noticed me playing.

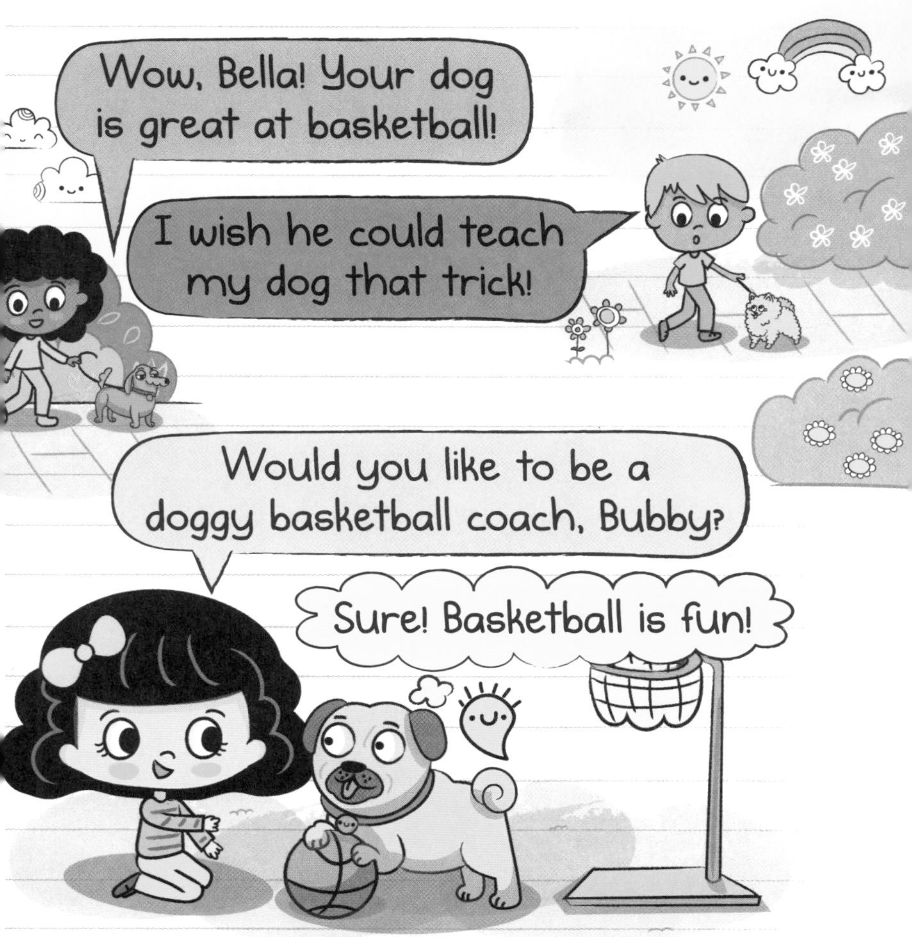
Wow, Bella! Your dog is great at basketball!
I wish he could teach my dog that trick!
Would you like to be a doggy basketball coach, Bubby?
Sure! Basketball is fun!

I've never coached before, Diary. But the other dogs are coming over tomorrow. I hope I'll do a good job!

Chapter 2

HOOPS AND SCOOPS

TUESDAY

Dear Diary,

Today after school, Bella's friends brought their dogs for their first basketball lesson.

Hi! I'm Bub.

I'm Frank.

And I'm Moxie. Let's do this!

I showed Frank and Moxie how to scoop and bop the ball.

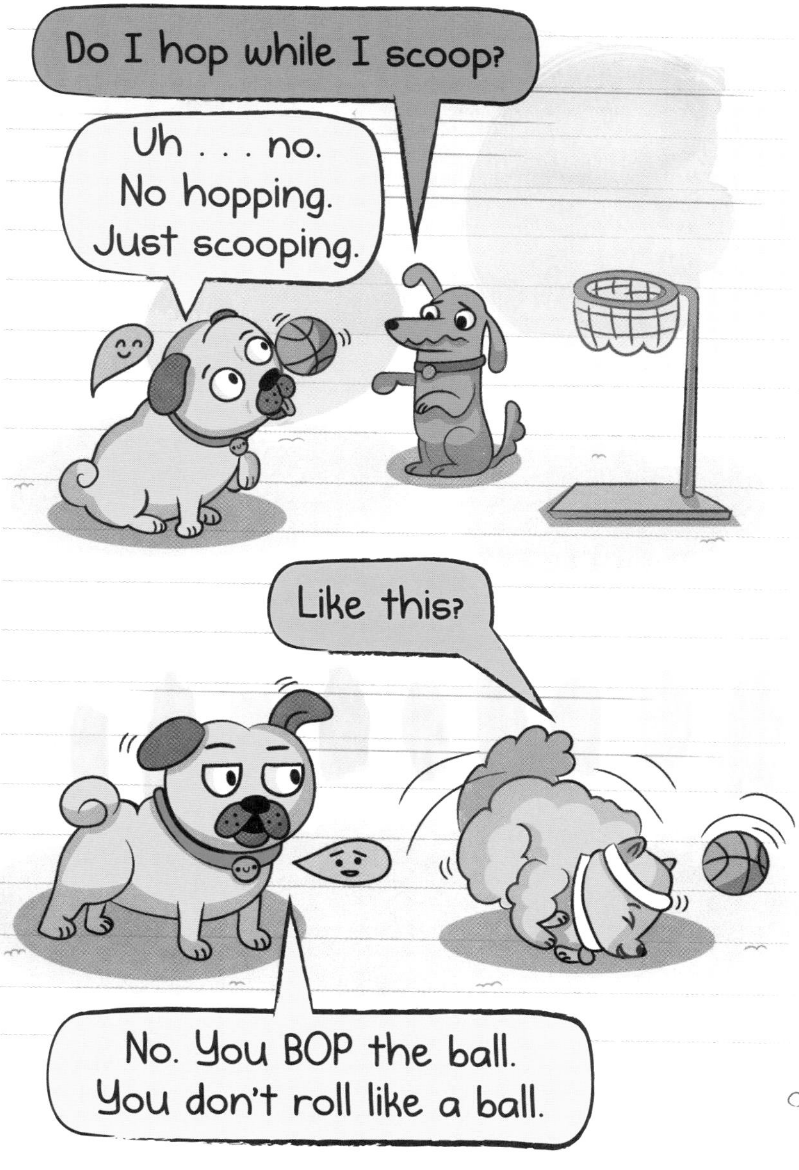
Do I hop while I scoop?
Uh . . . no.
No hopping.
Just scooping.
Like this?
No. You BOP the ball.
You don't roll like a ball.

Diary, coaching was harder than I thought!

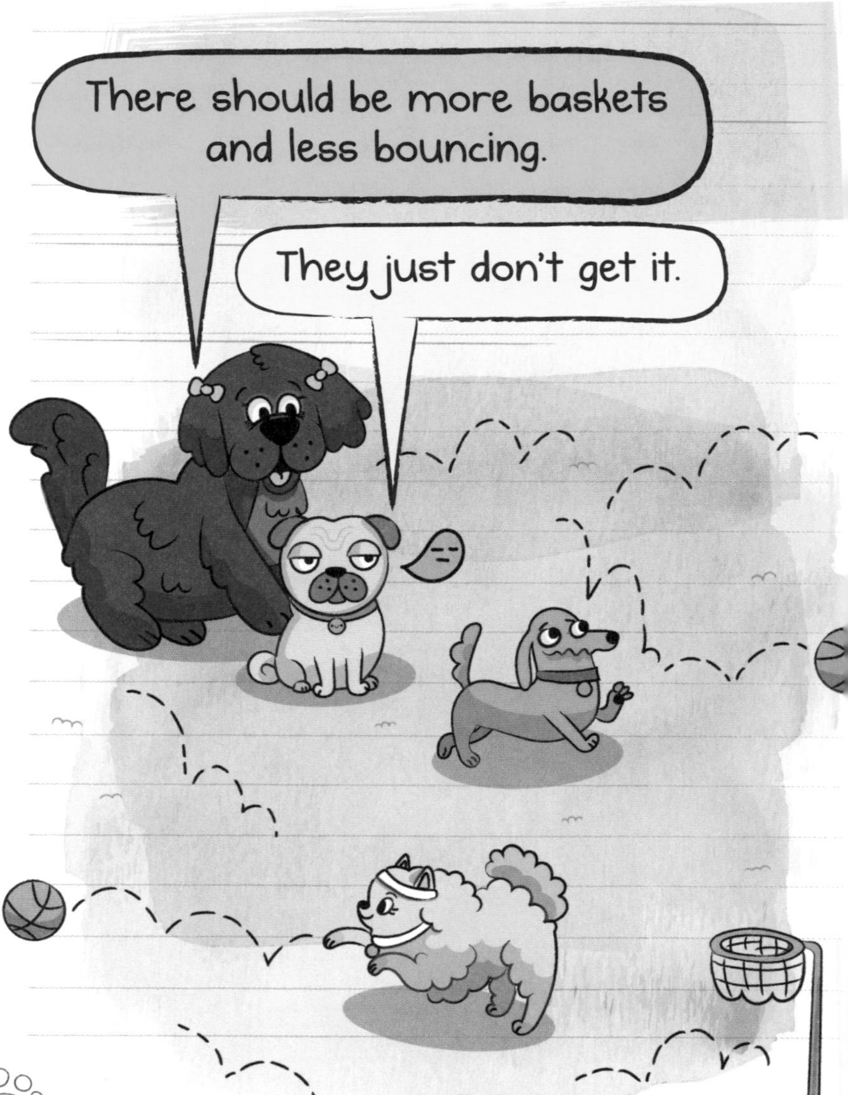
There should be more baskets and less bouncing.
They just don't get it.

I tried teaching Frank and Moxie again, nice and slow.

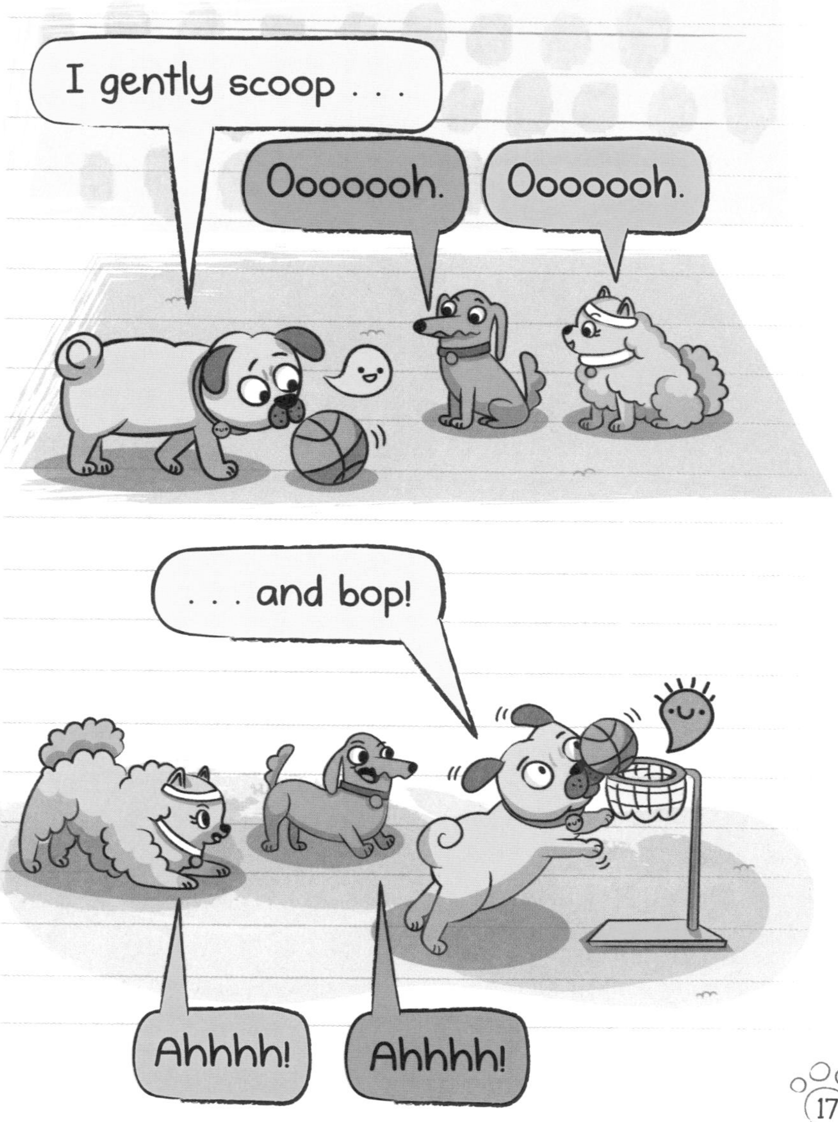
I gently scoop . . .
Ooooooh.
Ooooooh.
. . . and bop!
Ahhhh!
Ahhhh!

After a couple of practice shots, they finally each made a basket!

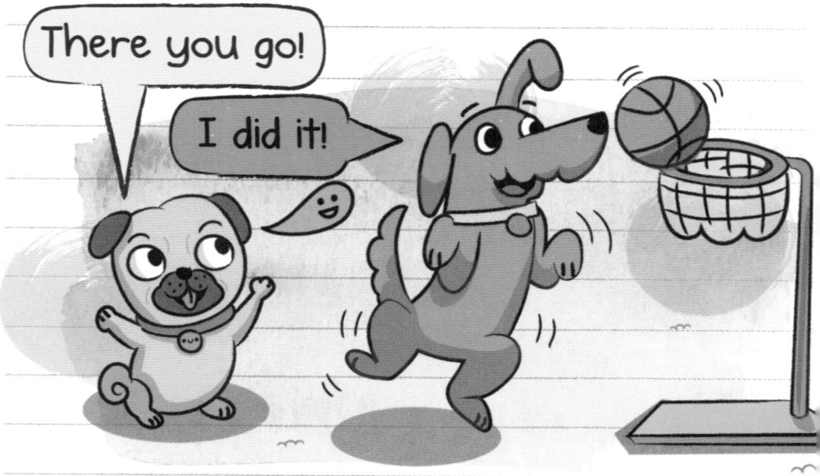
There you go!
I did it!

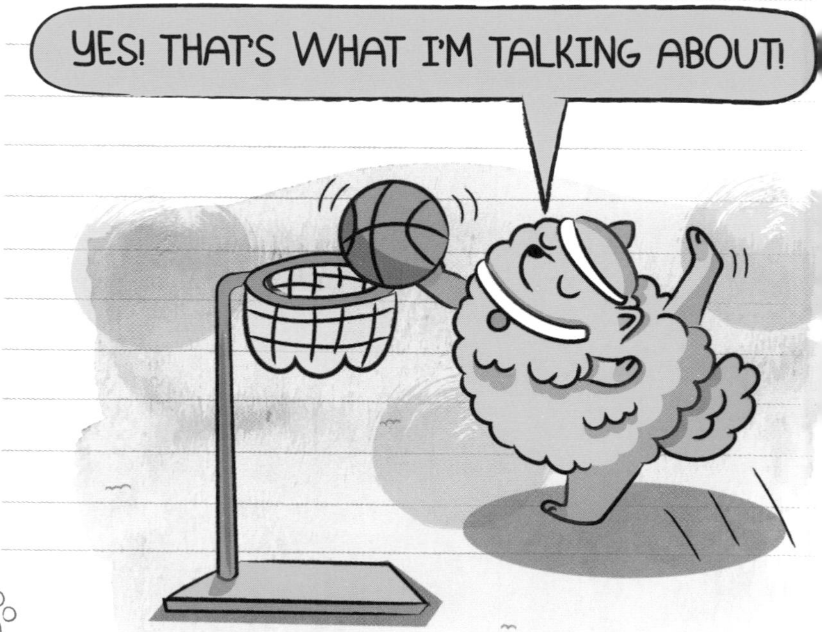
YES! THAT'S WHAT I'M TALKING ABOUT!

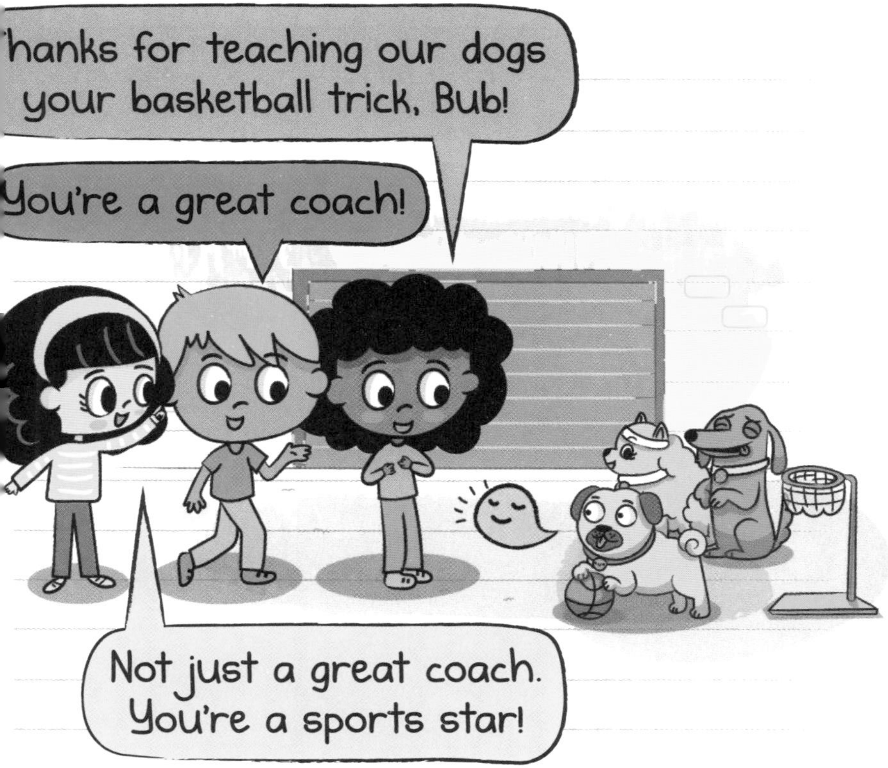
hanks for teaching our dogs your basketball trick, Bub!
You're a great coach!
Not just a great coach. You're a sports star!

That was when Bella had an idea. A big, bopping basketball idea that would change everything.

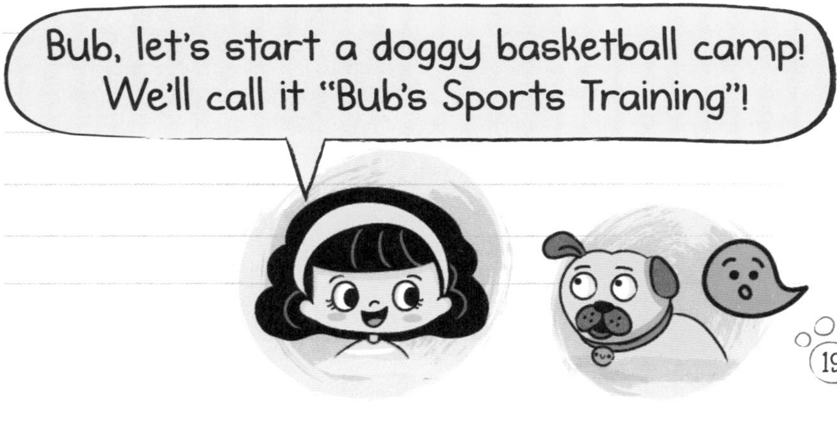
Bub, let's start a doggy basketball camp! We'll call it "Bub's Sports Training"!

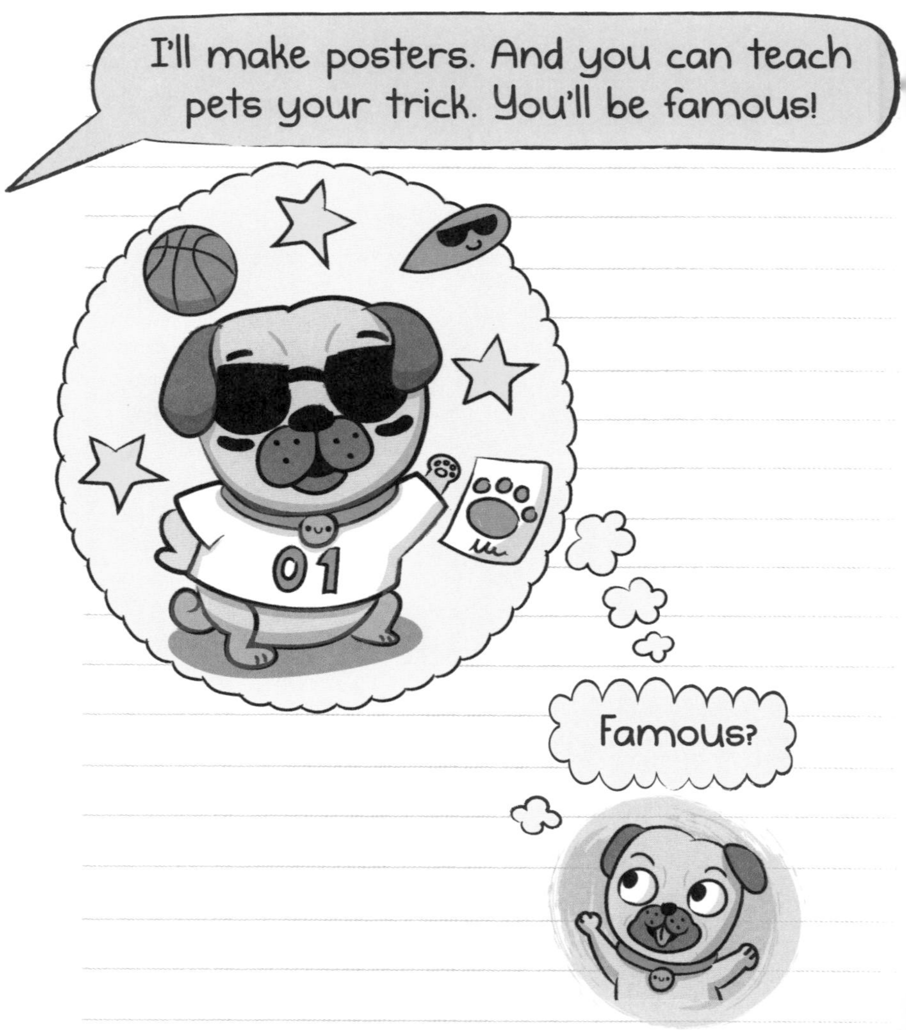
I'll make posters. And you can teach pets your trick. You'll be famous!
01
Famous?

I've seen famous people on TV. They wear sunglasses and sign autographs. Could that be me, Diary? Could I be . . . famous?

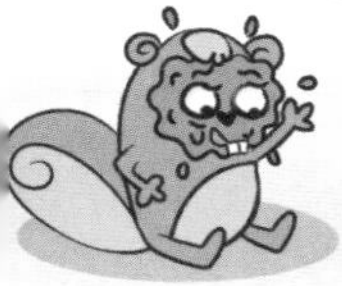

Chapter 3

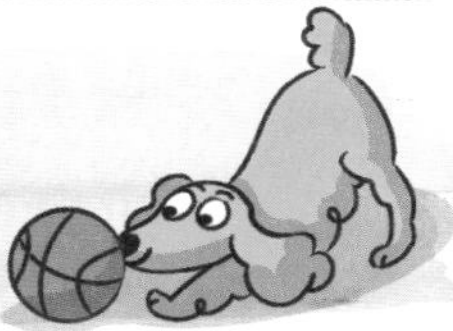

JUMPING THROUGH HOOPS

WEDNESDAY

Dear Diary,

Last night Bella and I painted signs for Bub's Sports Training.

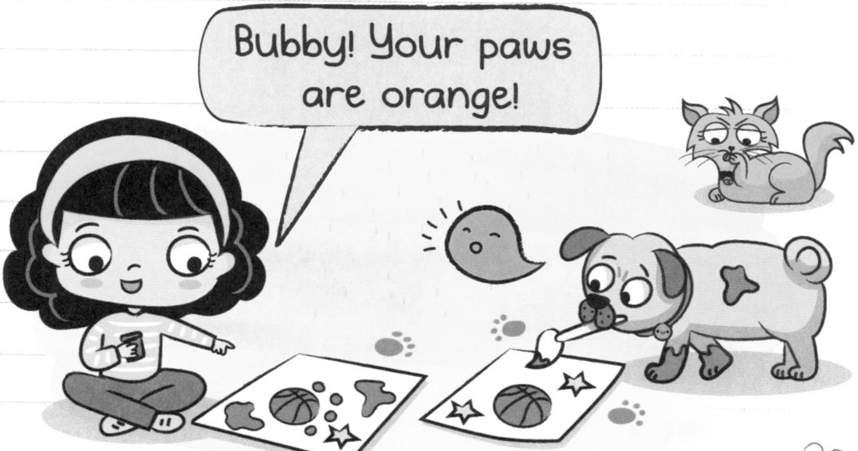
Bubby! Your paws are orange!

She hung the signs up at school and said everyone was interested!

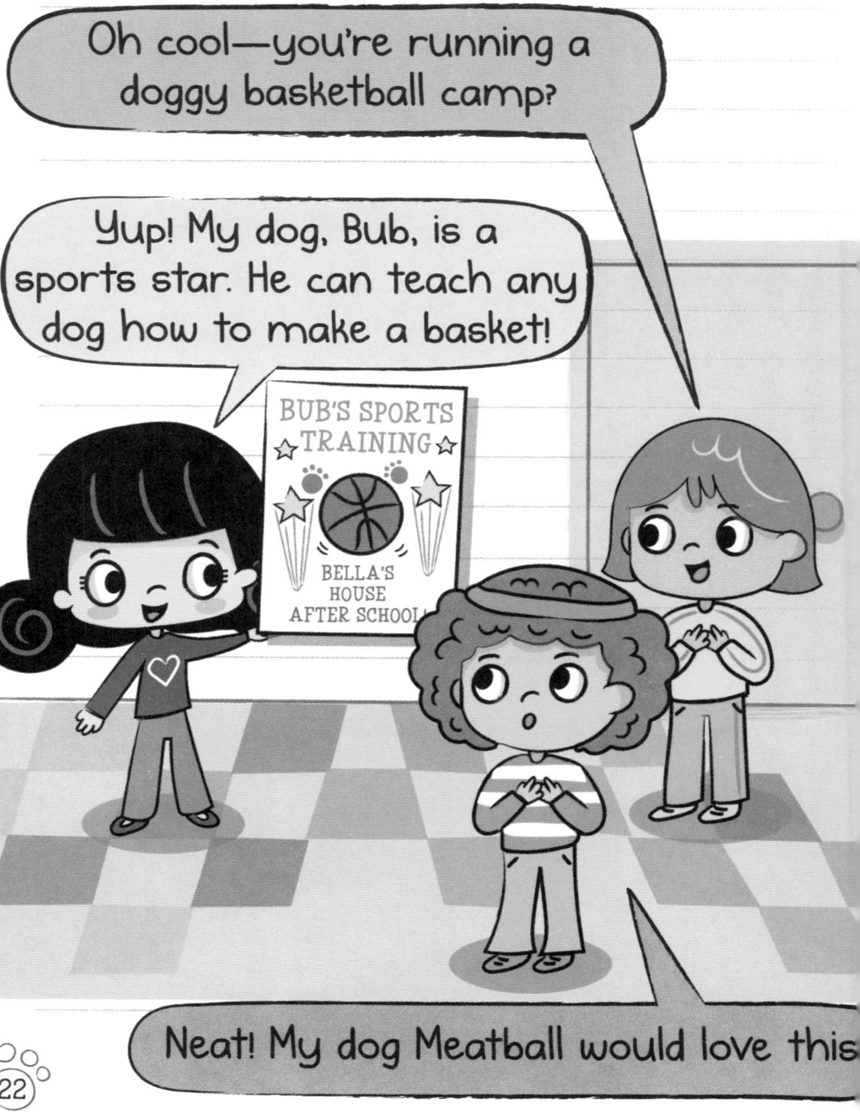
Oh cool—you're running a doggy basketball camp?
Yup! My dog, Bub, is a sports star. He can teach any dog how to make a basket!
BUB'S SPORTS TRAINING
BELLA'S HOUSE AFTER SCHOOL!
Neat! My dog Meatball would love this

When Bella got home, there were a bunch of dogs waiting for the training session to begin. I was excited!

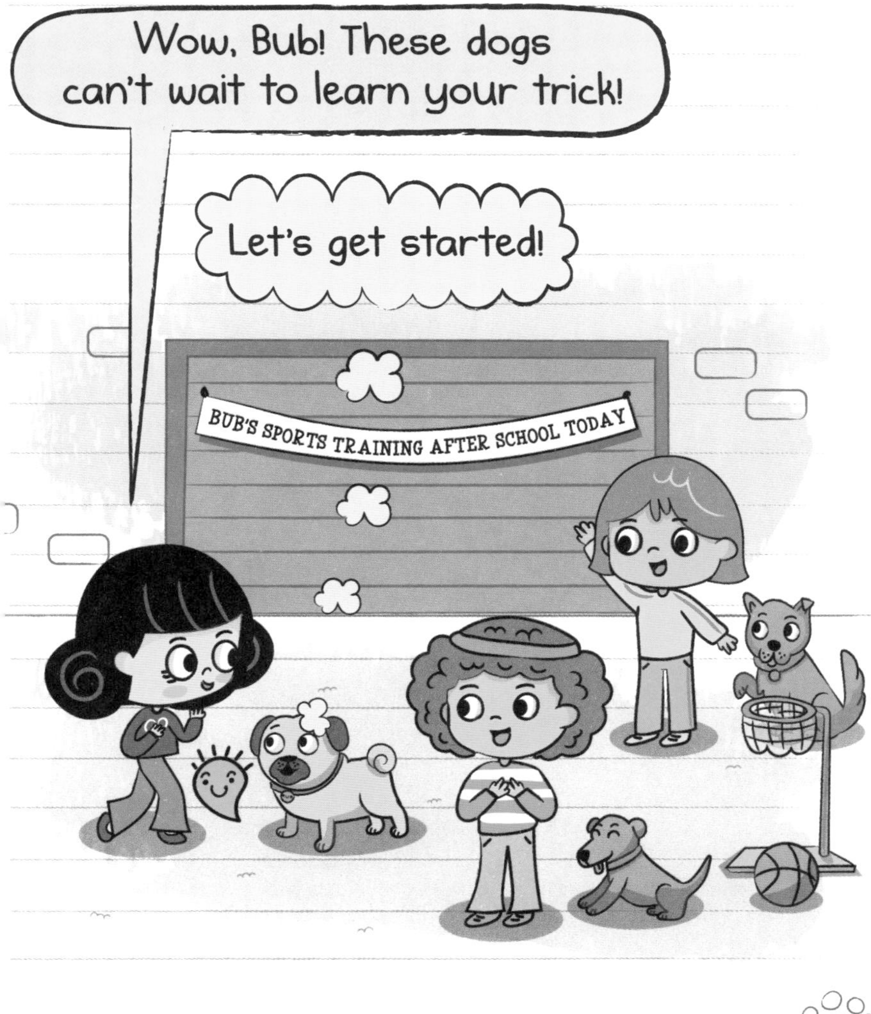
Wow, Bub! These dogs can't wait to learn your trick!
Let's get started!
BUB'S SPORTS TRAINING AFTER SCHOOL TODAY

I went nice and slow, just like I had when I taught Frank and Moxie. I figured it would work with these dogs, too.

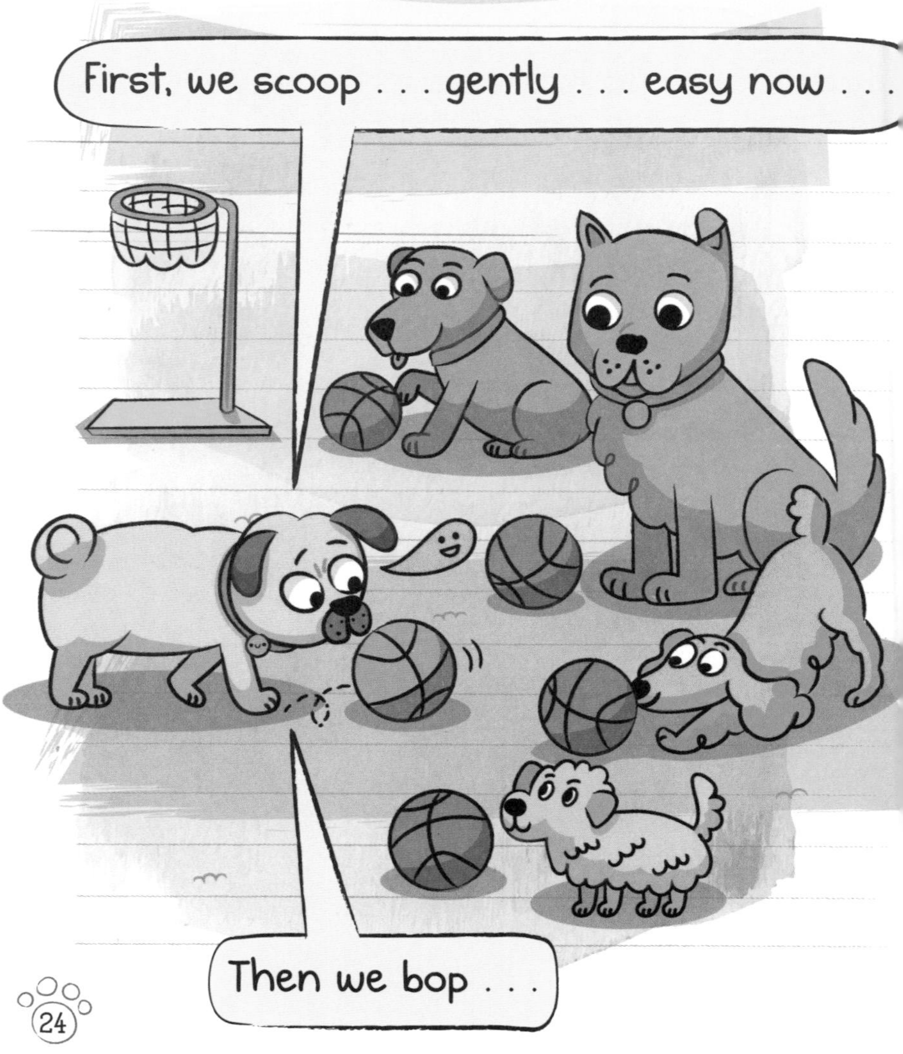
First, we scoop . . . gently . . . easy now . . .
Then we bop . . .

But I was wrong.

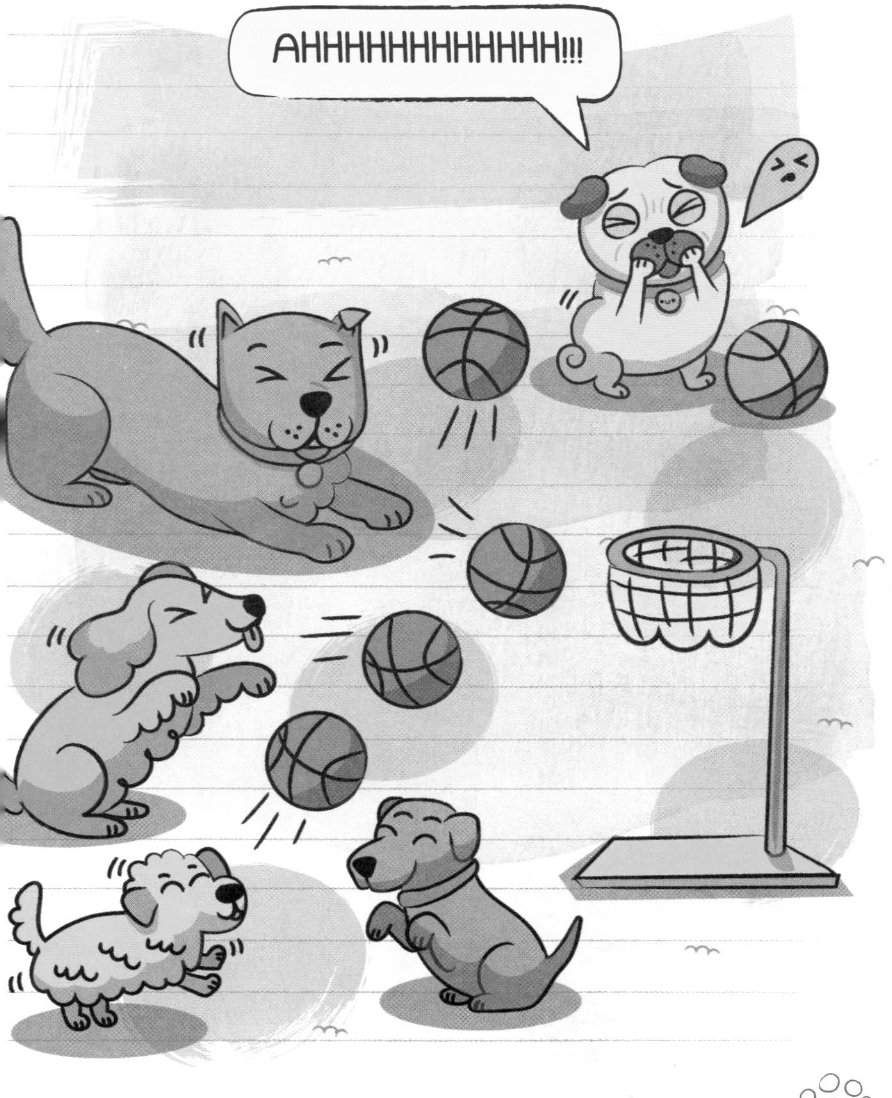
AHHHHHHHHHHHHH!!!

Today's basketball training was wild! There were so many dogs. And each one needed help with something different.

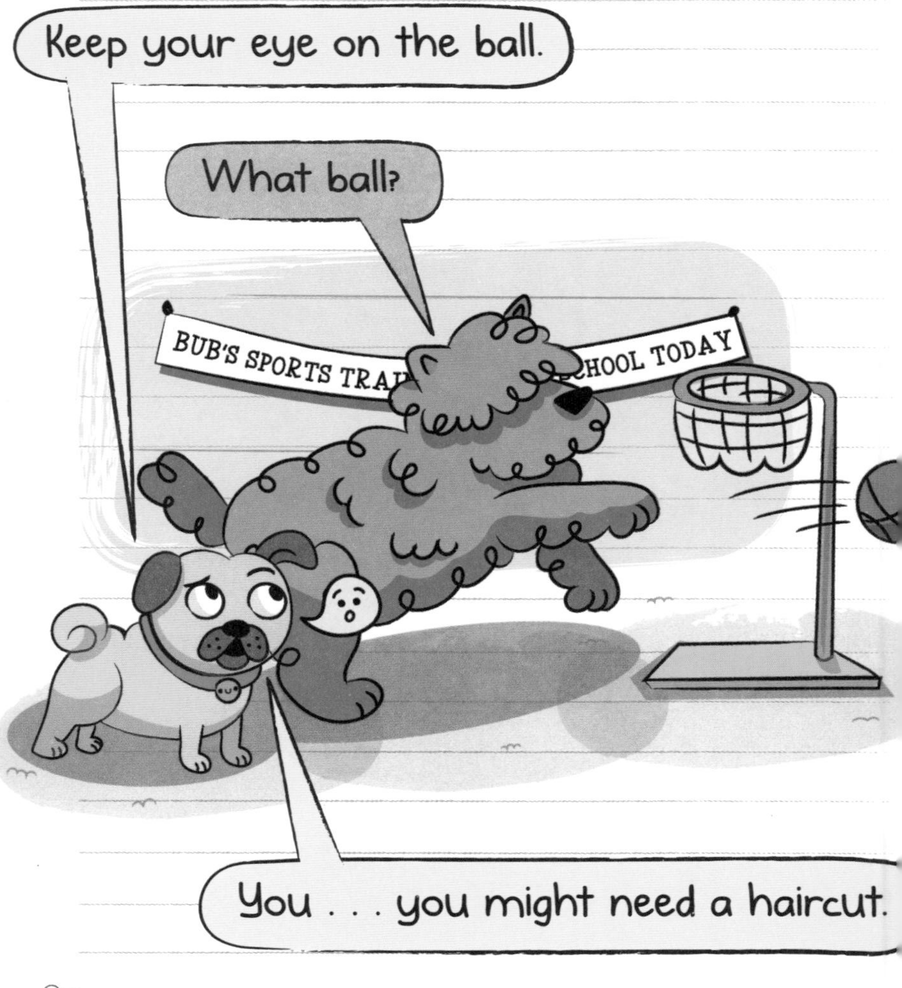
Keep your eye on the ball.
What ball?
BUB'S SPORTS TRA
CHOOL TODAY
You . . . you might need a haircut.

I was running out of energy!

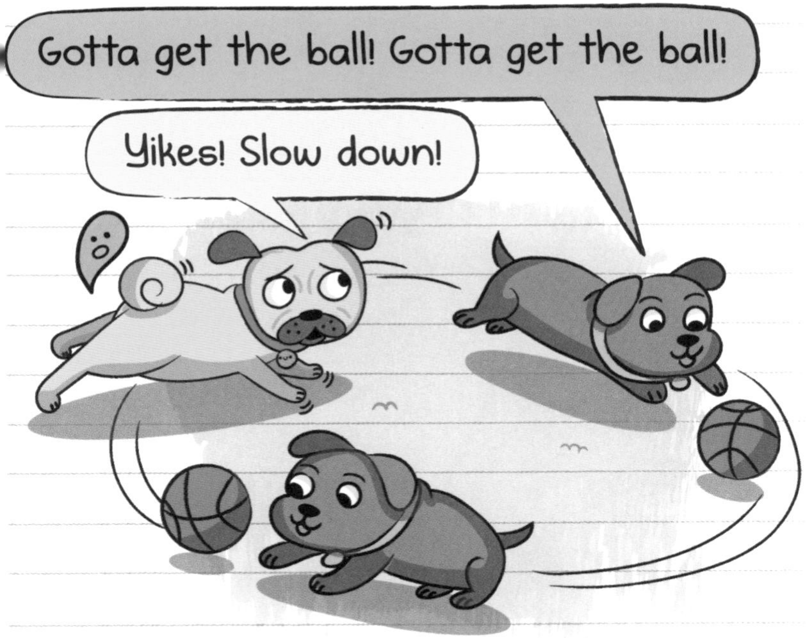
Gotta get the ball! Gotta get the ball!
Yikes! Slow down!

But every time a new dog learned my trick, I felt super proud!

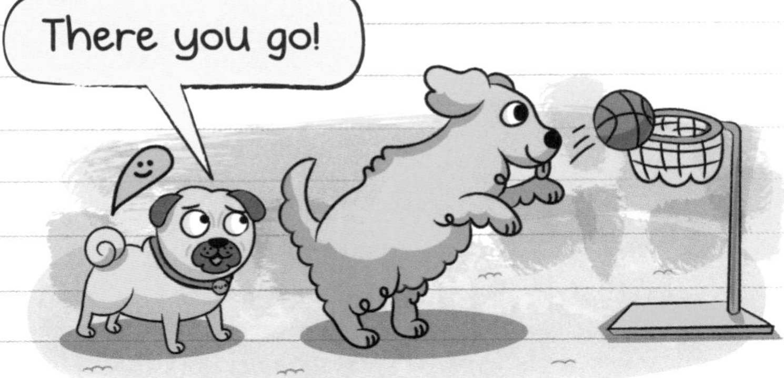
There you go!

And I kept reminding myself that I was making Bella proud, too. So, I didn't mind chasing after the ball. For the fiftieth tim

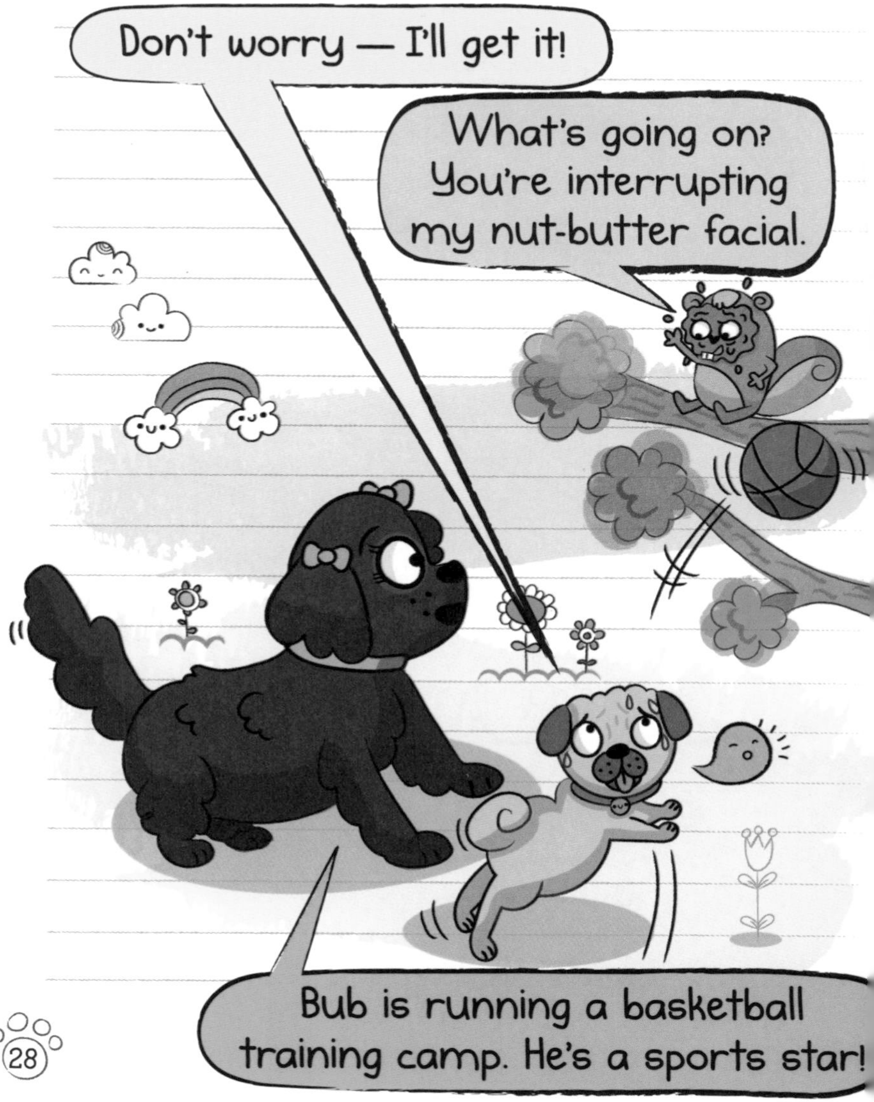
Don't worry — I'll get it!
What's going on? You're interrupting my nut-butter facial.
Bub is running a basketball training camp. He's a sports star!

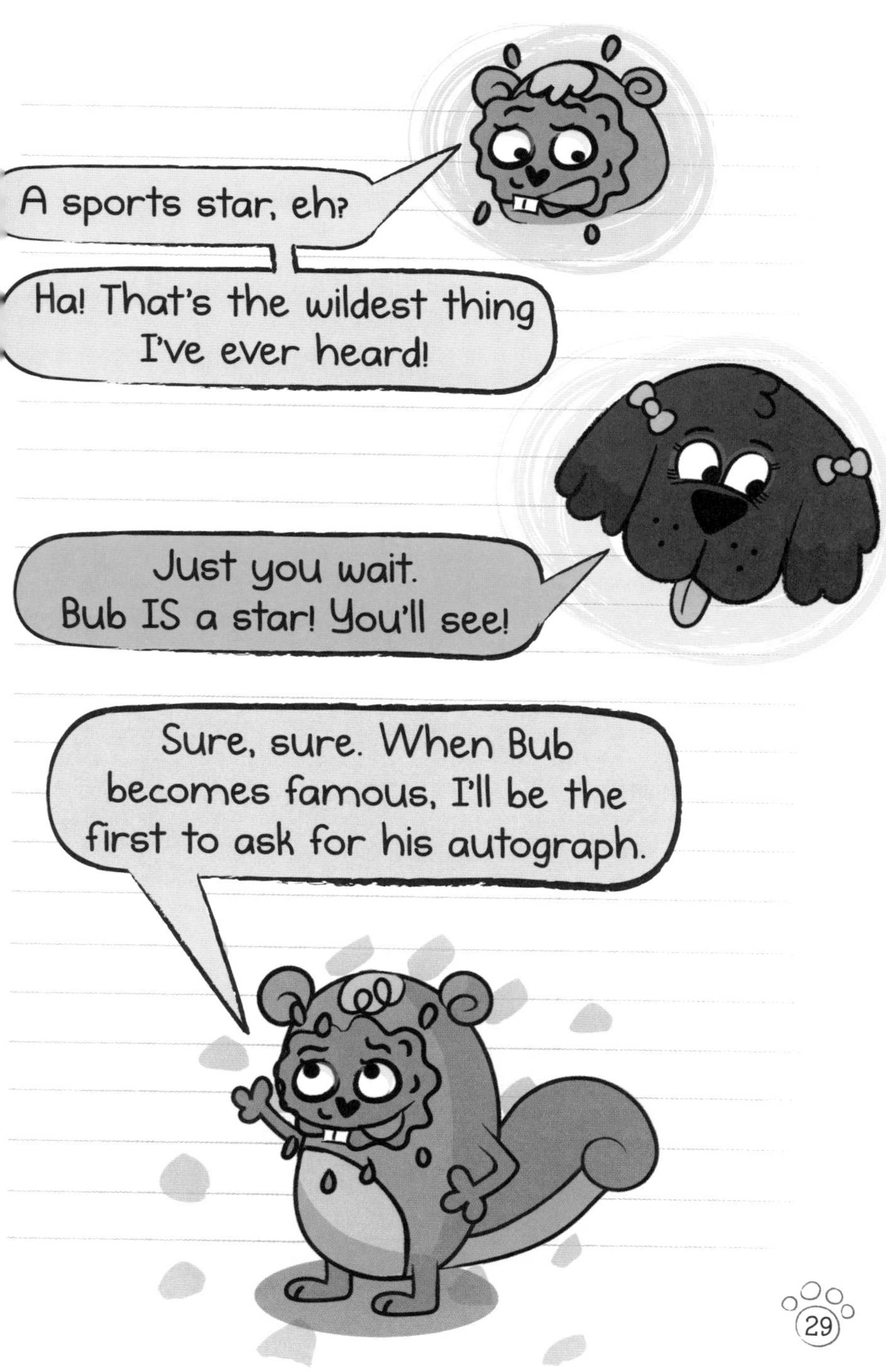
A sports star, eh?
Ha! That's the wildest thing I've ever heard!
Just you wait. Bub IS a star! You'll see!
Sure, sure. When Bub becomes famous, I'll be the first to ask for his autograph.

It took all afternoon, but finally, every dog had learned my trick. Kind of.

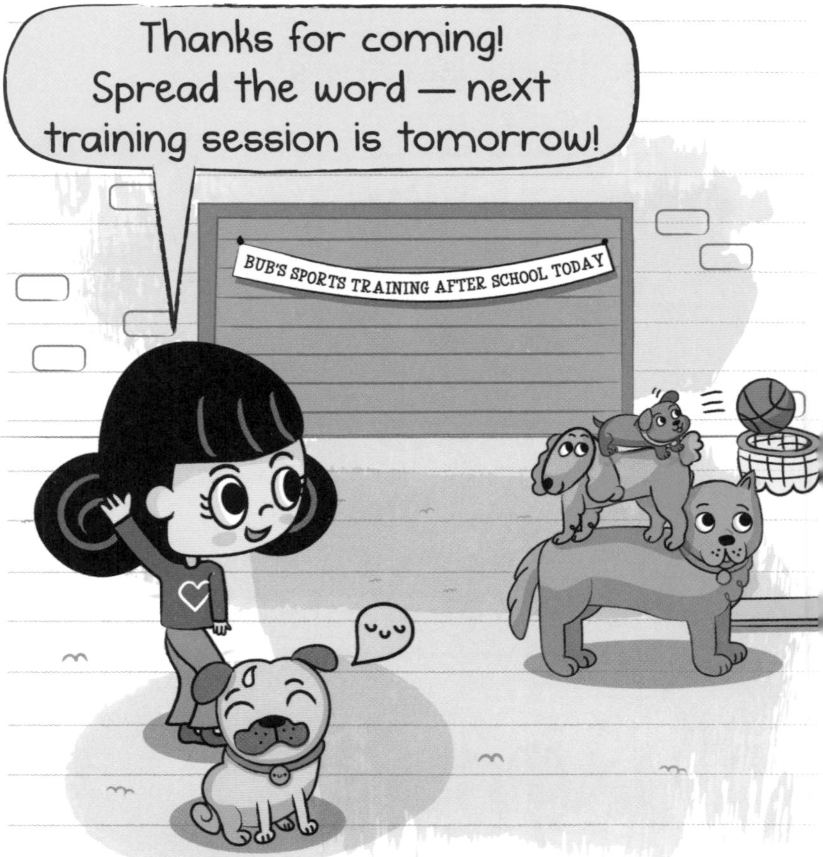
Thanks for coming! Spread the word — next training session is tomorrow!
BUB'S SPORTS TRAINING AFTER SCHOOL TODAY

Today was a huge success! I felt great! And so tired. Do you think tomorrow's training will be calmer?

Chapter 4

SPORTS-STAR HOOPLA

THURSDAY

Dear Diary,

When Bella got home from school, I was ready for another training session.

I made you a jersey in art class! You'll look like a real sports star now!

SPORTS SUPERSTAR

But when we went outside . . .

. . . I saw that word had spread. To Every. Single. Dog. In. Town.

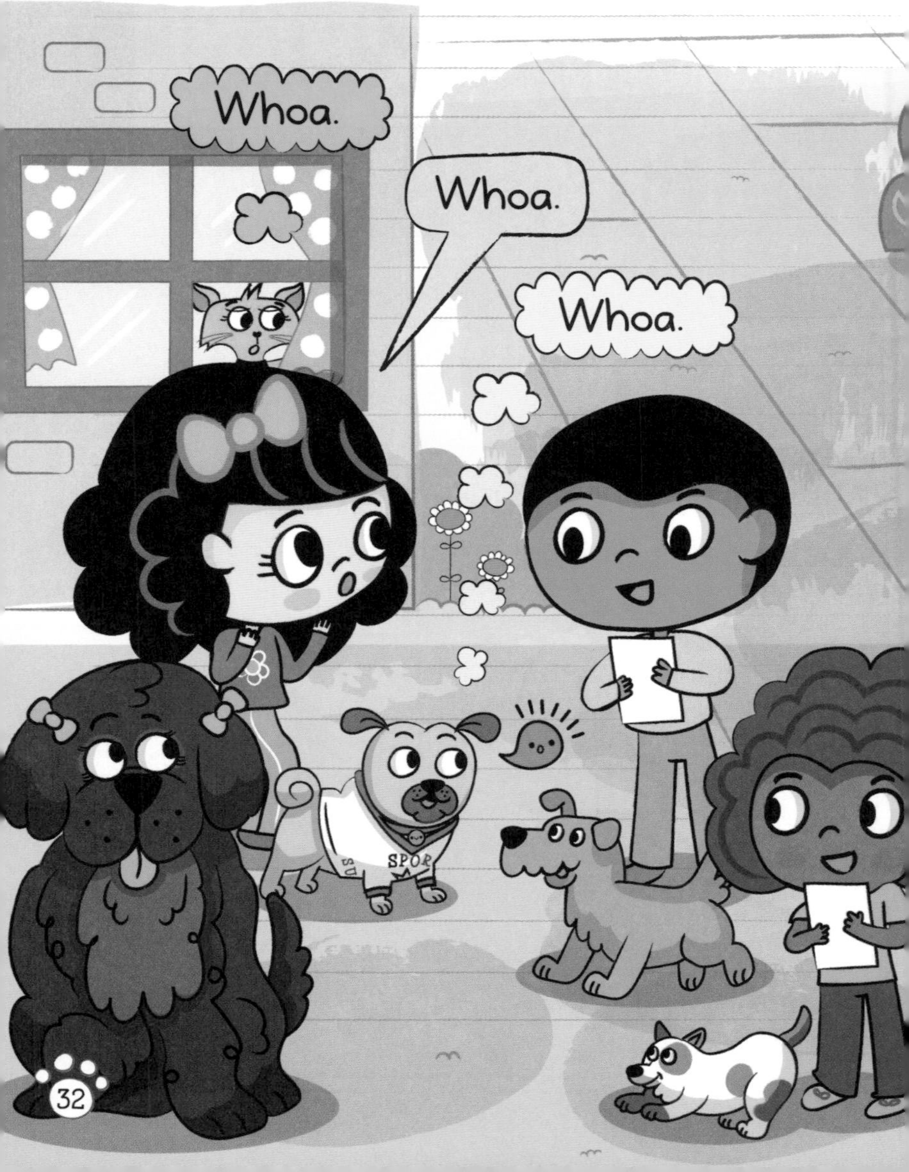

Whoa.
Whoa.
Whoa.

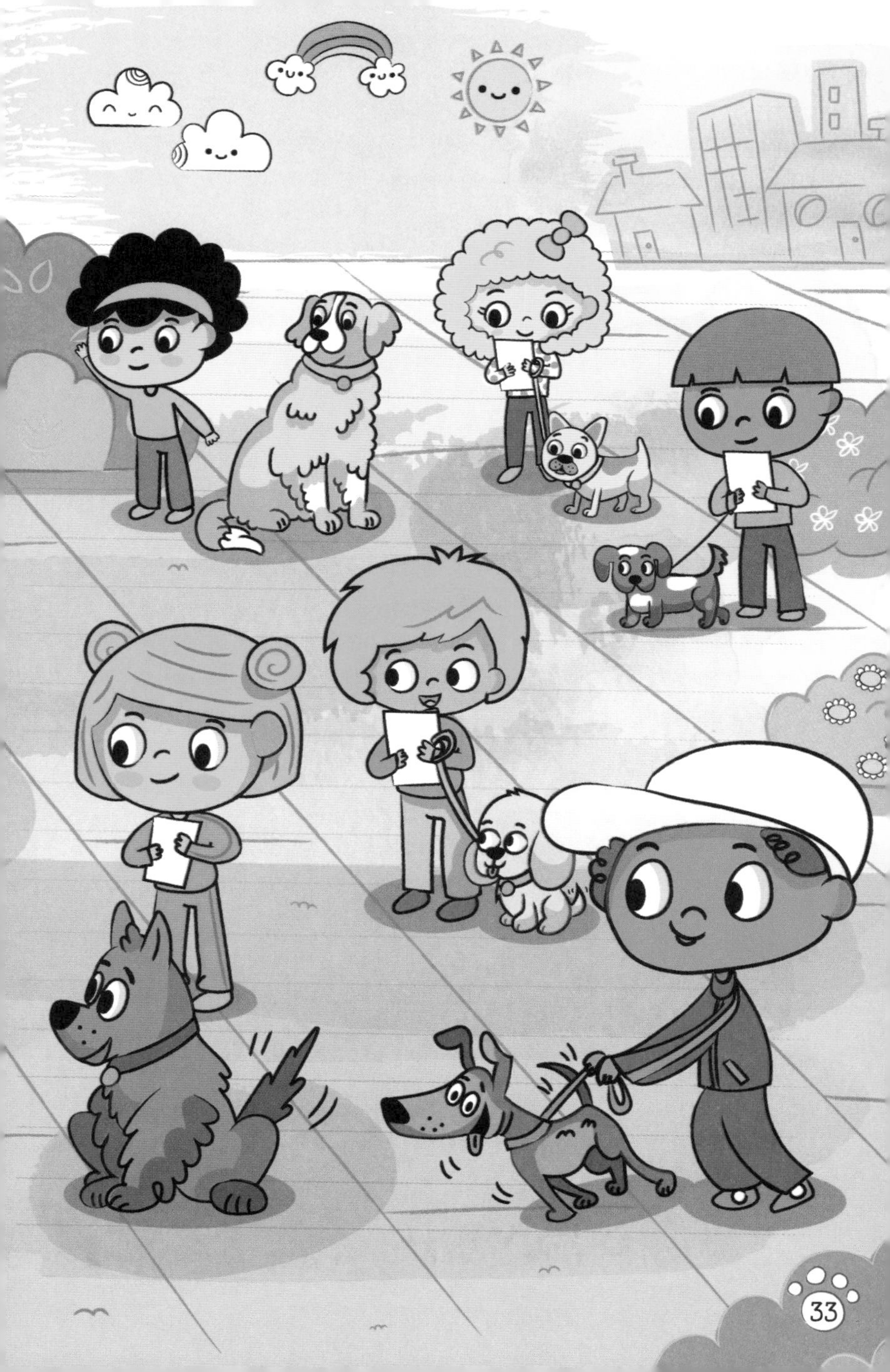

I tried my best to keep up.

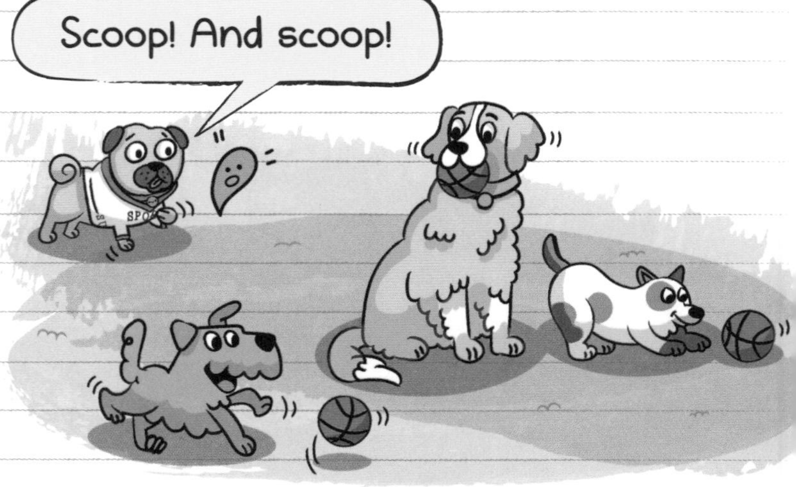
Scoop! And scoop!
SPO

But there were just too many dogs.

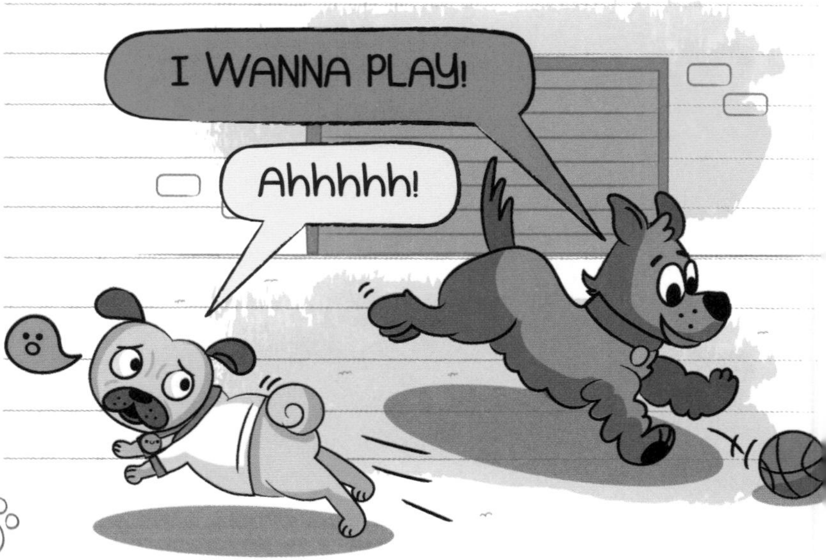
I WANNA PLAY!
Ahhhhh!

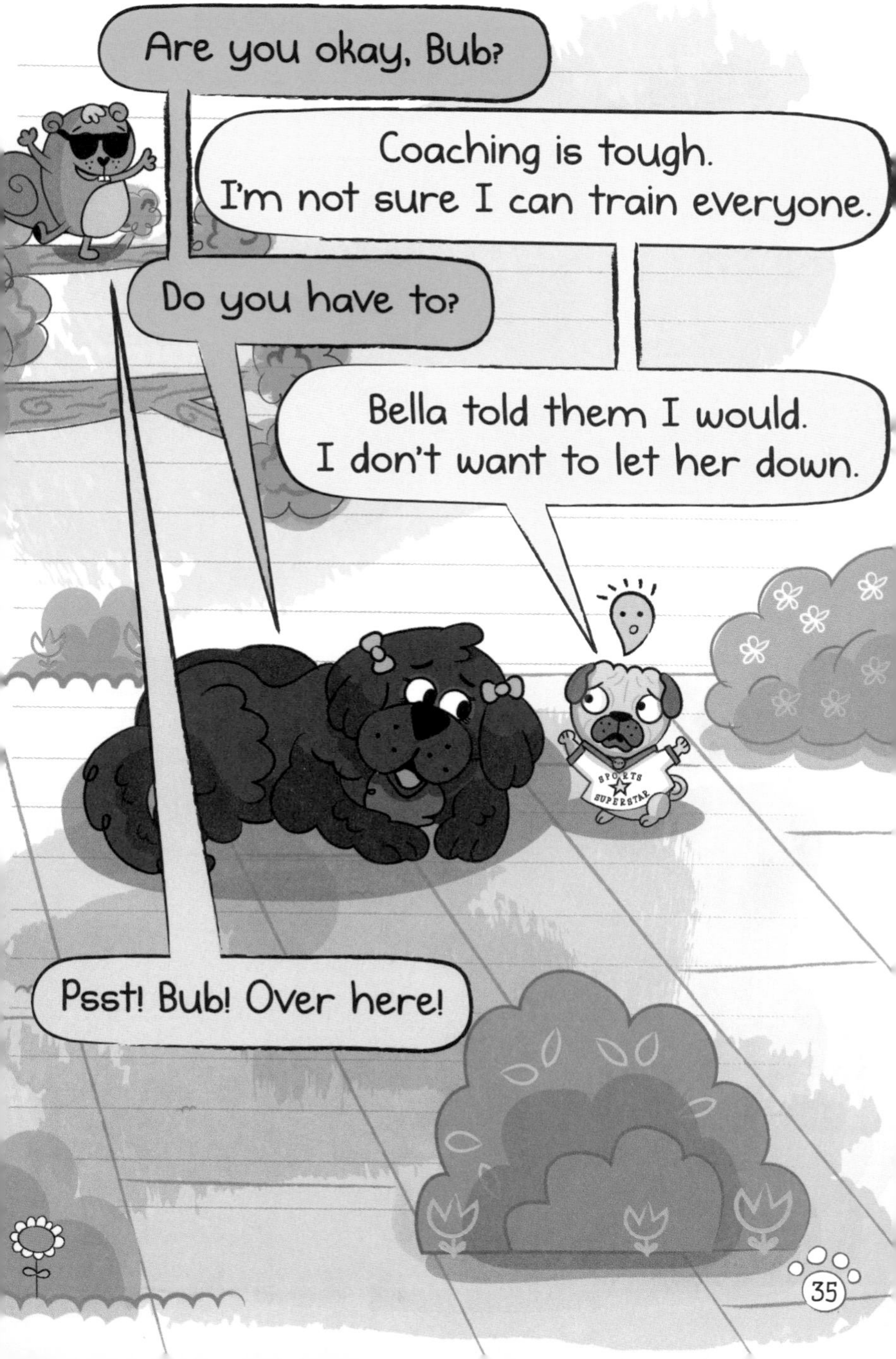
Are you okay, Bub?
Coaching is tough. I'm not sure I can train everyone.
Do you have to?
Bella told them I would. I don't want to let her down.
Psst! Bub! Over here!
SPORTS SUPERSTAR

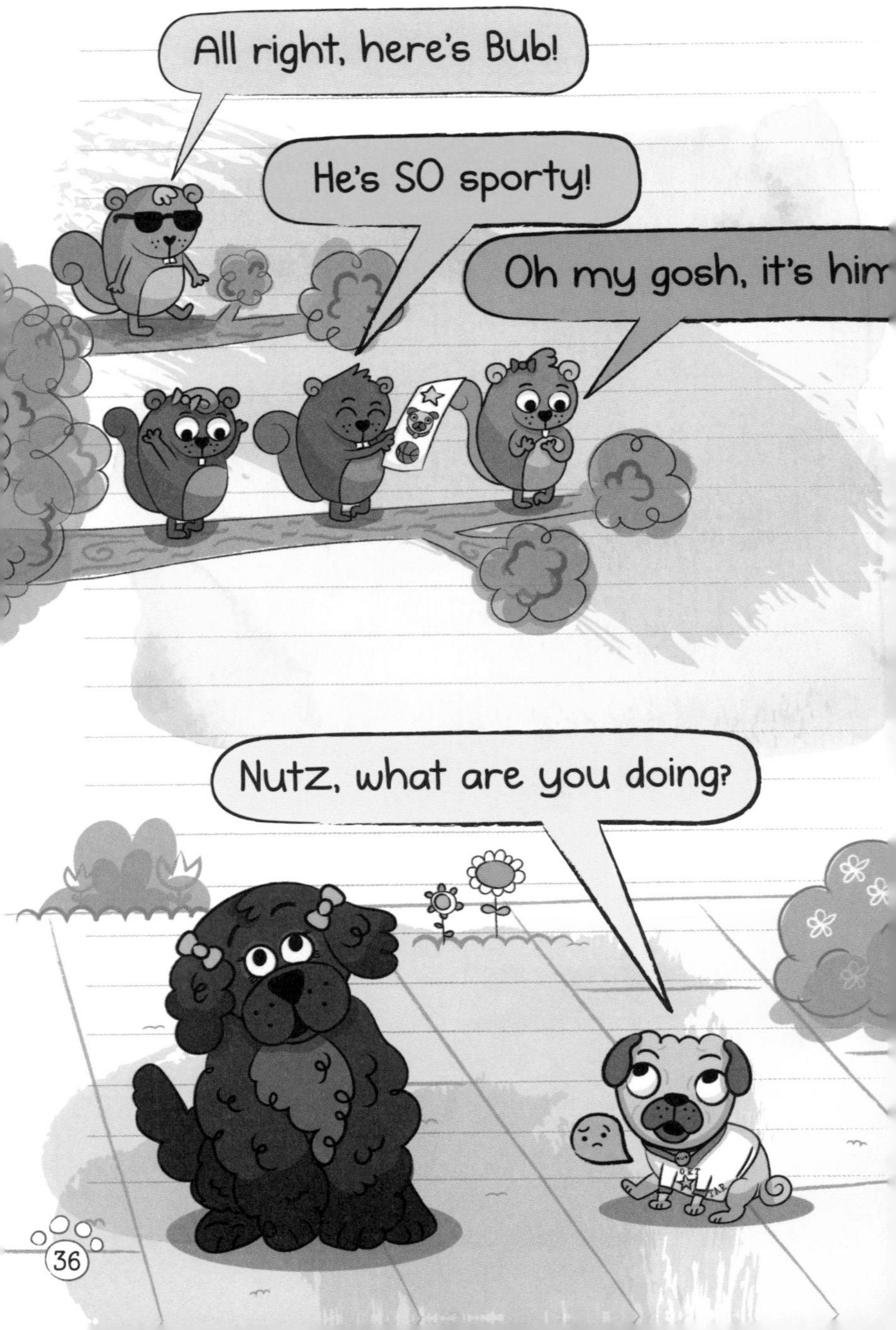
All right, here's Bub!
He's SO sporty!
Oh my gosh, it's him
Nutz, what are you doing?

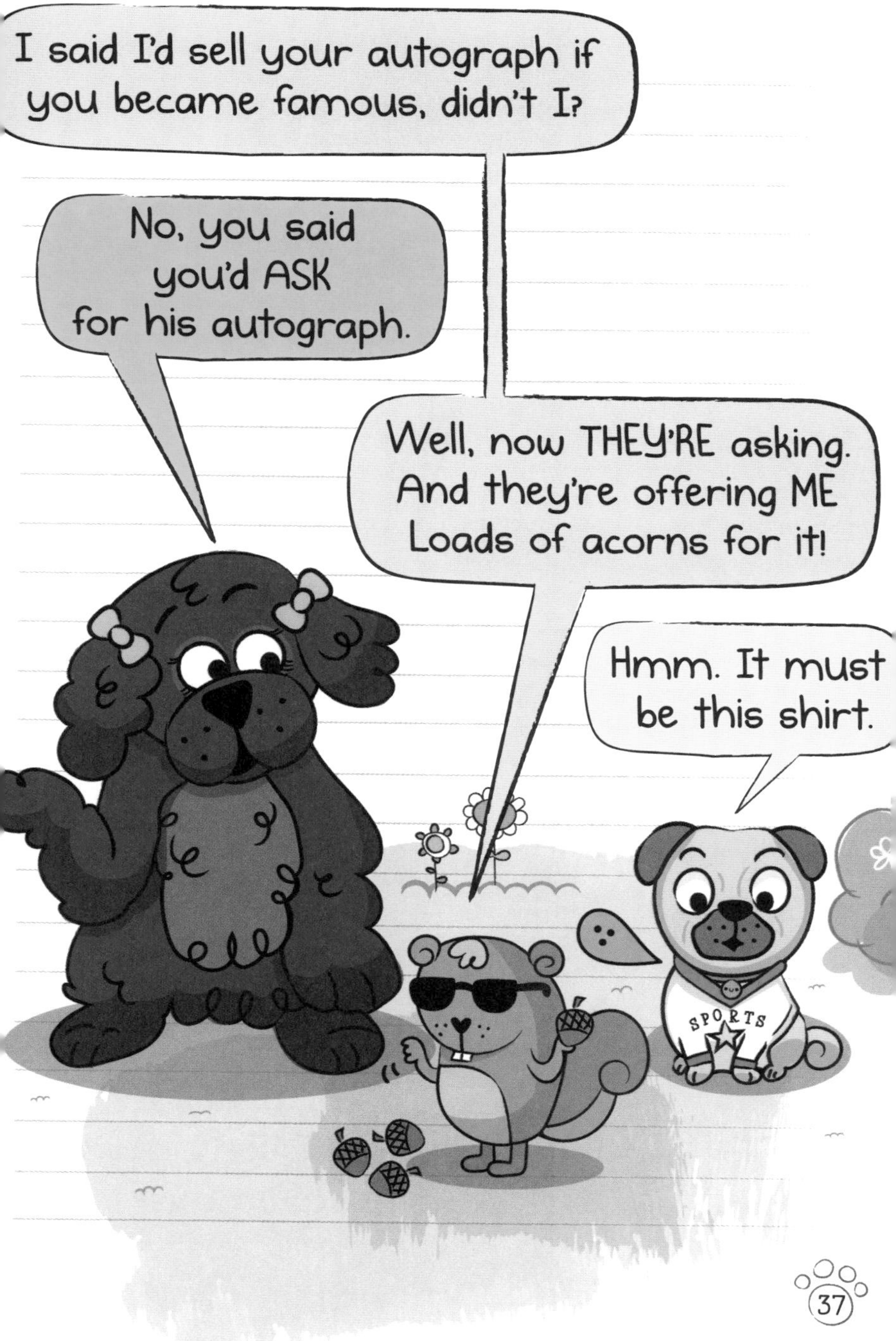
I said I'd sell your autograph if you became famous, didn't I?
No, you said you'd ASK for his autograph.
Well, now THEY'RE asking. And they're offering ME Loads of acorns for it!
Hmm. It must be this shirt.
SPORTS

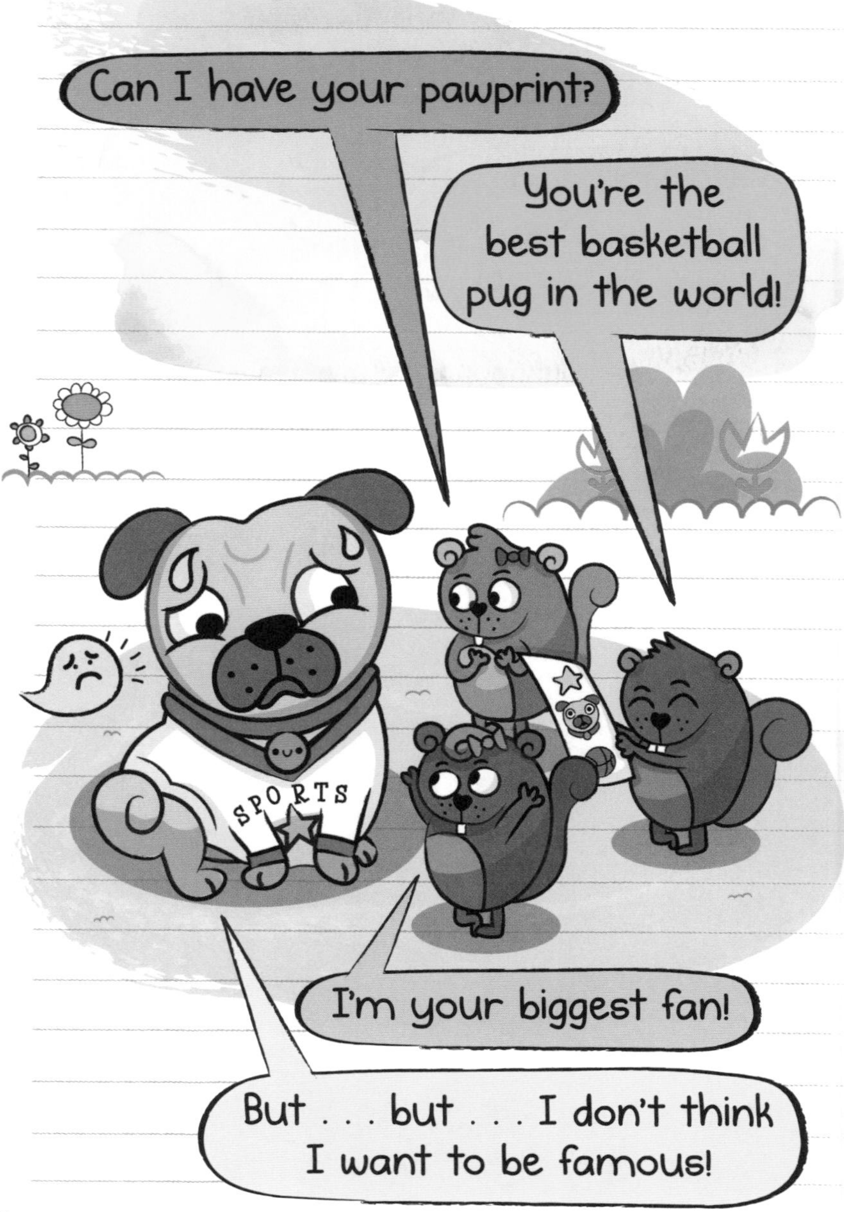
Can I have your pawprint?
You're the best basketball pug in the world!
SPORTS
I'm your biggest fan!
But . . . but . . . I don't think I want to be famous!

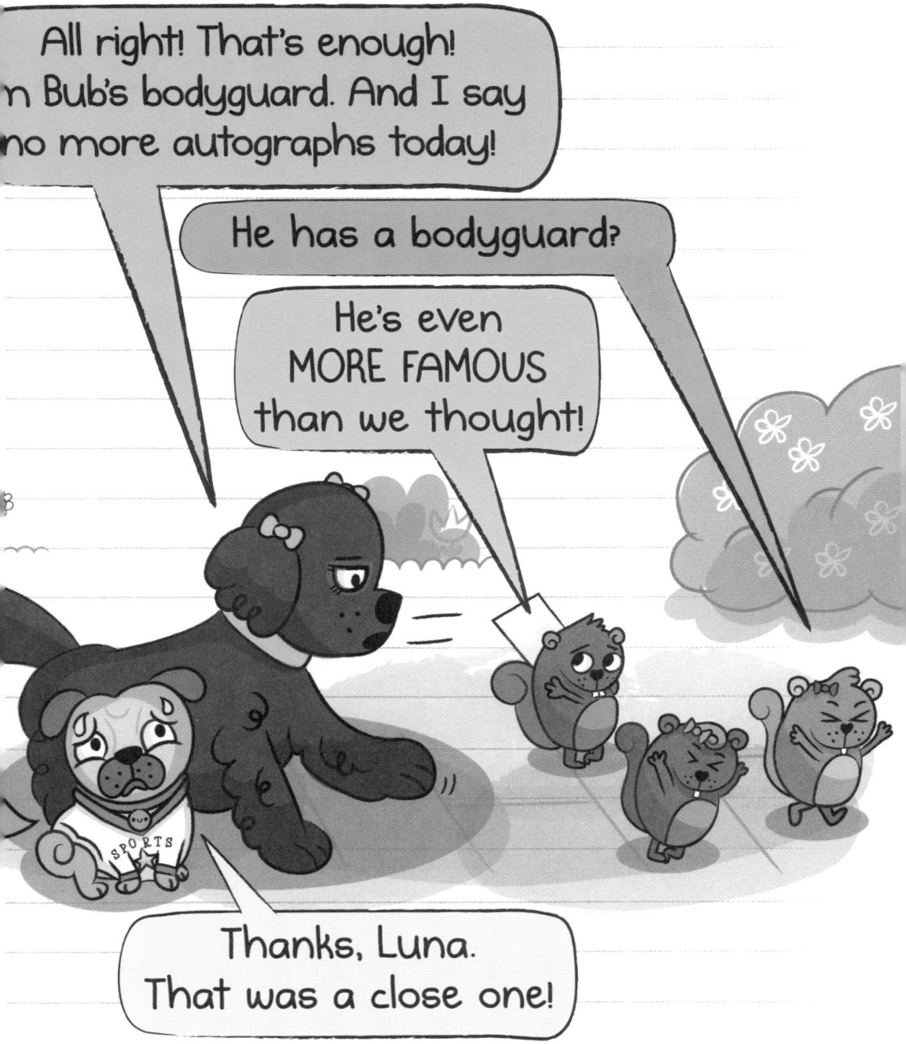
All right! That's enough!
n Bub's bodyguard. And I say
no more autographs today!
He has a bodyguard?
He's even
MORE FAMOUS
than we thought!
Thanks, Luna.
That was a close one!

I don't know, Diary. I really like basketball. But I'm not sure being a sports star is all it's cracked up to be.

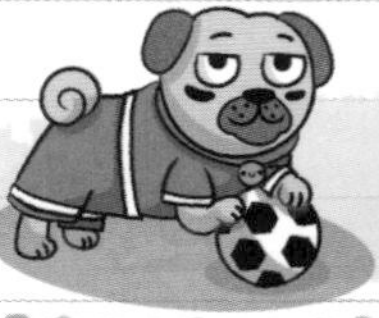

Chapter 5

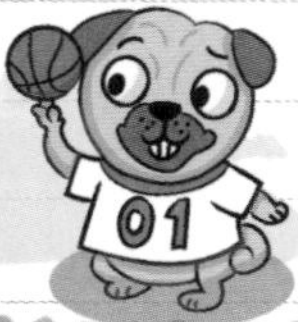

HOOPING INTO THE SPOTLIGHT

FRIDAY

Dear Diary,

Bella cancelled today's training session. I think she realized it was too much.

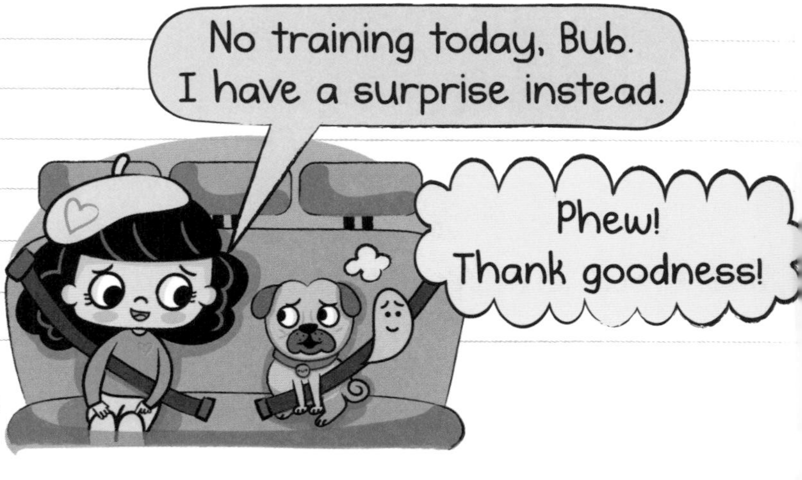
No training today, Bub. I have a surprise instead.
Phew! Thank goodness!

Bella's mom drove us to a photography studio downtown.

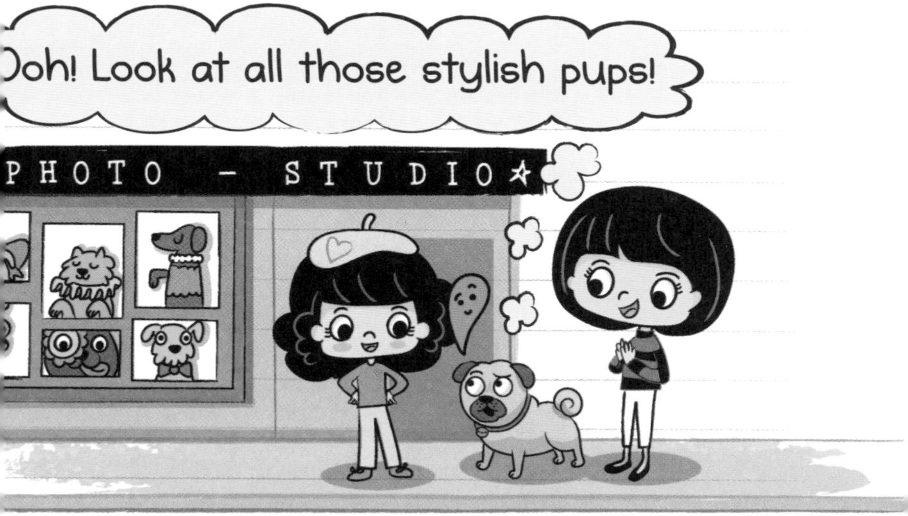
Ooh! Look at all those stylish pups!
PHOTO - STUDIO

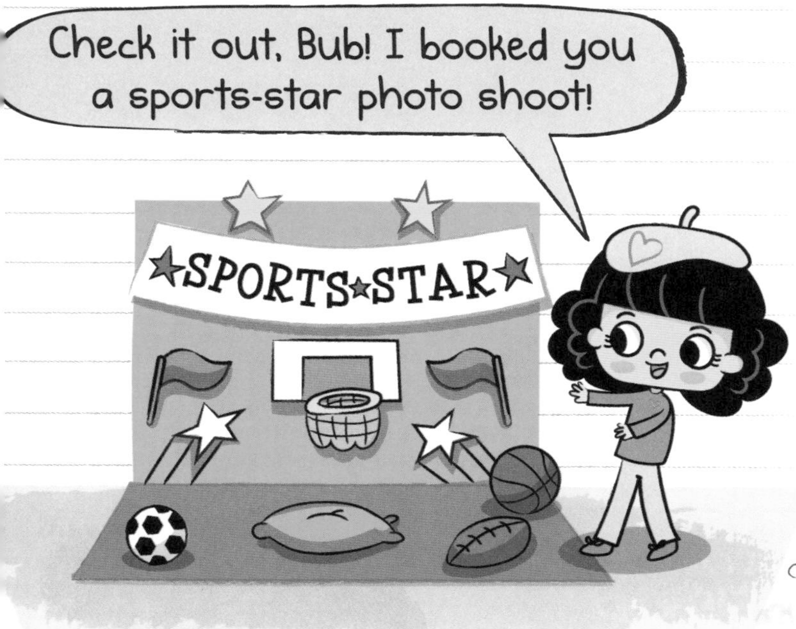
Check it out, Bub! I booked you a sports-star photo shoot!
SPORTS STAR

Now THIS was the kind of sports star stuff I could get into, Diary! I loved posing! And the camera loved me!

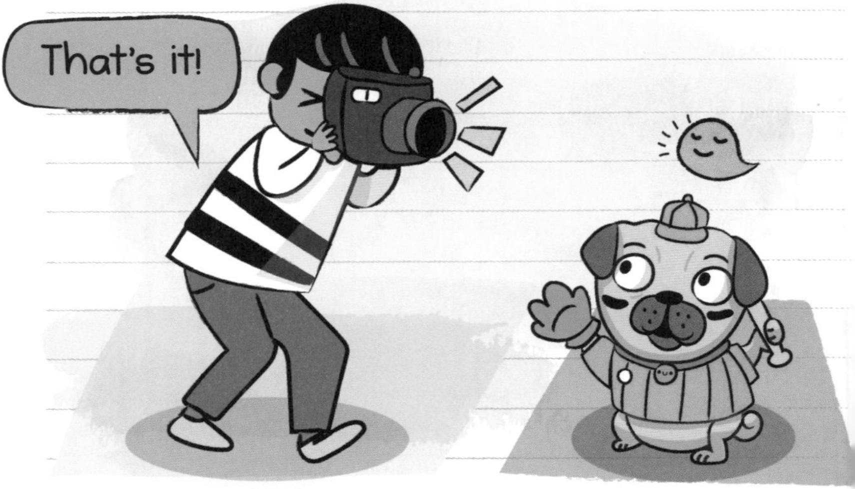
That's it!

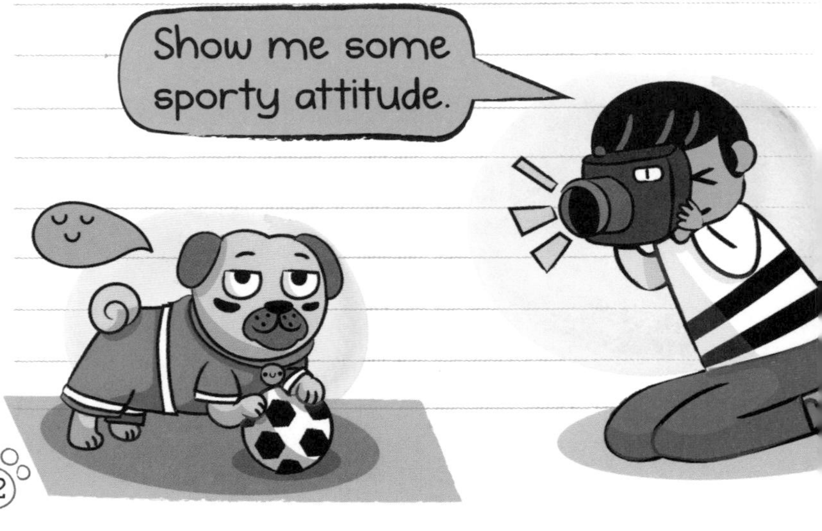
Show me some sporty attitude.

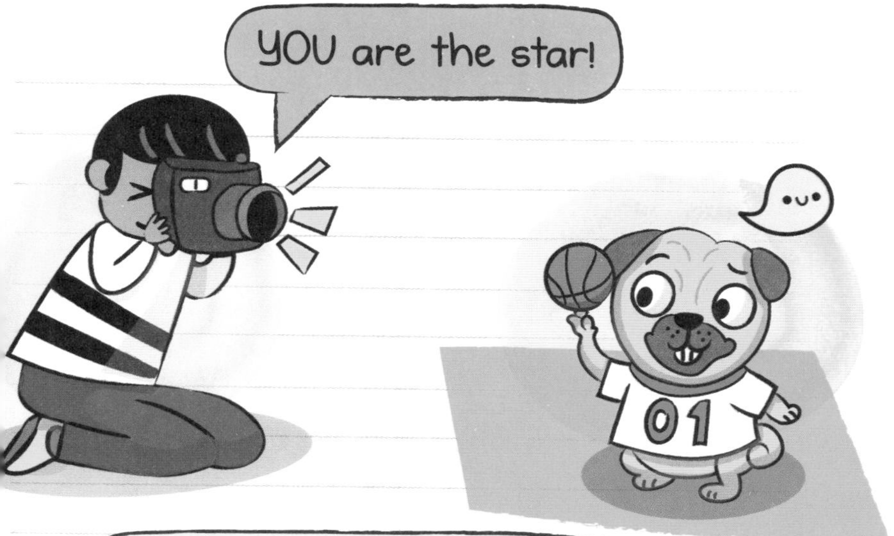
YOU are the star!
01

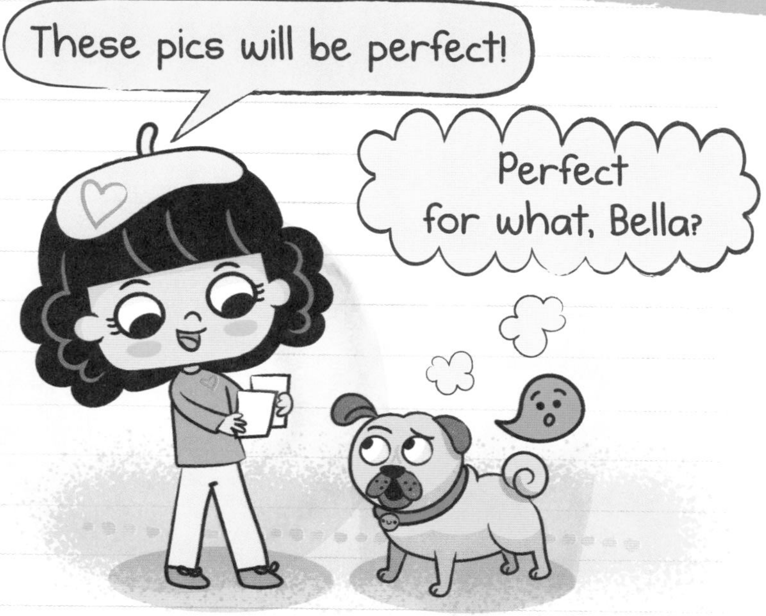
These pics will be perfect!
Perfect for what, Bella?

Diary, we left the photography studio with our photos.

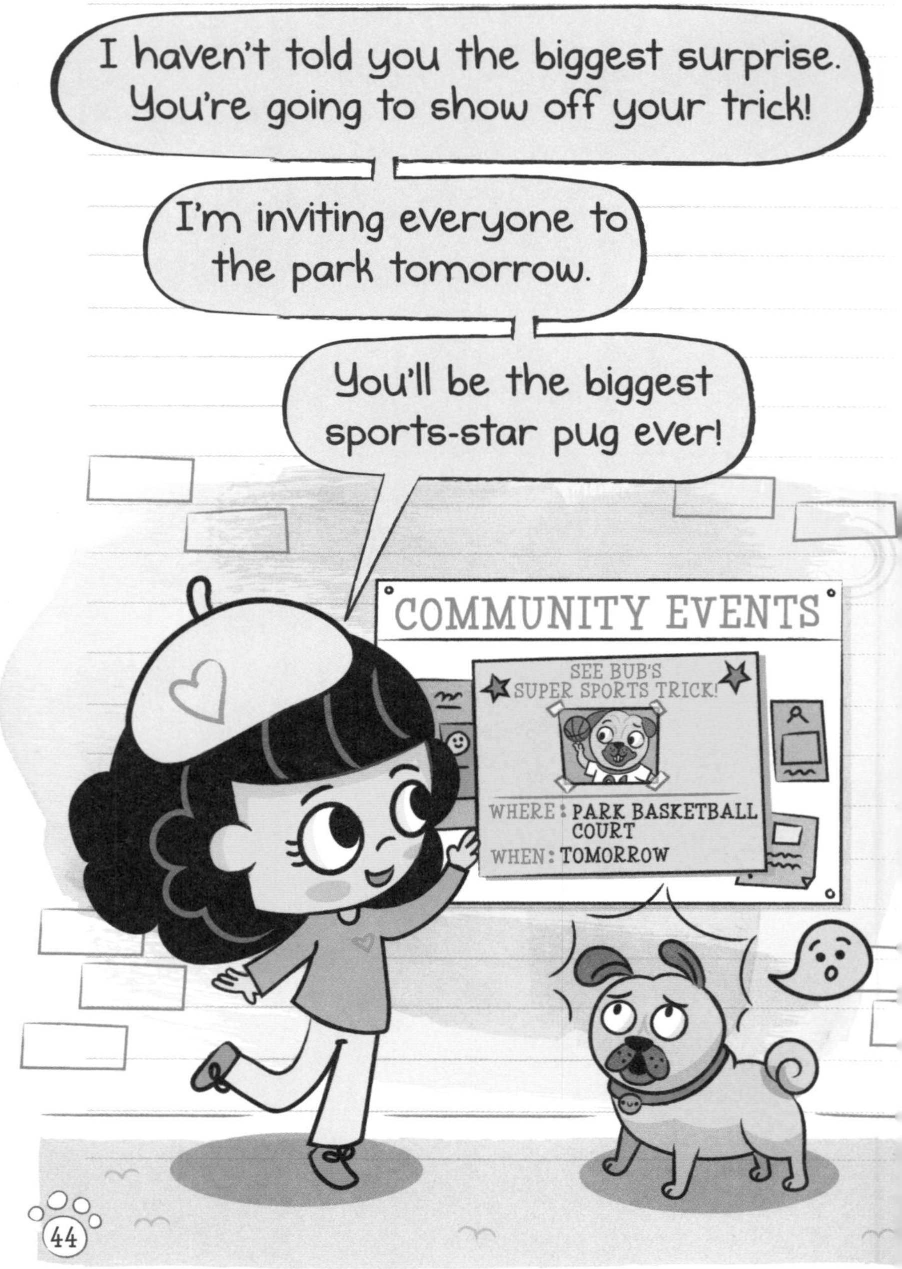
I haven't told you the biggest surprise. You're going to show off your trick!
I'm inviting everyone to the park tomorrow.
You'll be the biggest sports-star pug ever!
COMMUNITY EVENTS
SEE BUB'S SUPER SPORTS TRICK!
WHERE: PARK BASKETBALL COURT
WHEN: TOMORROW

Diary, Bella was so sure I could do it. But I was nervous! Just thinking about performing in front of everyone made me toot!

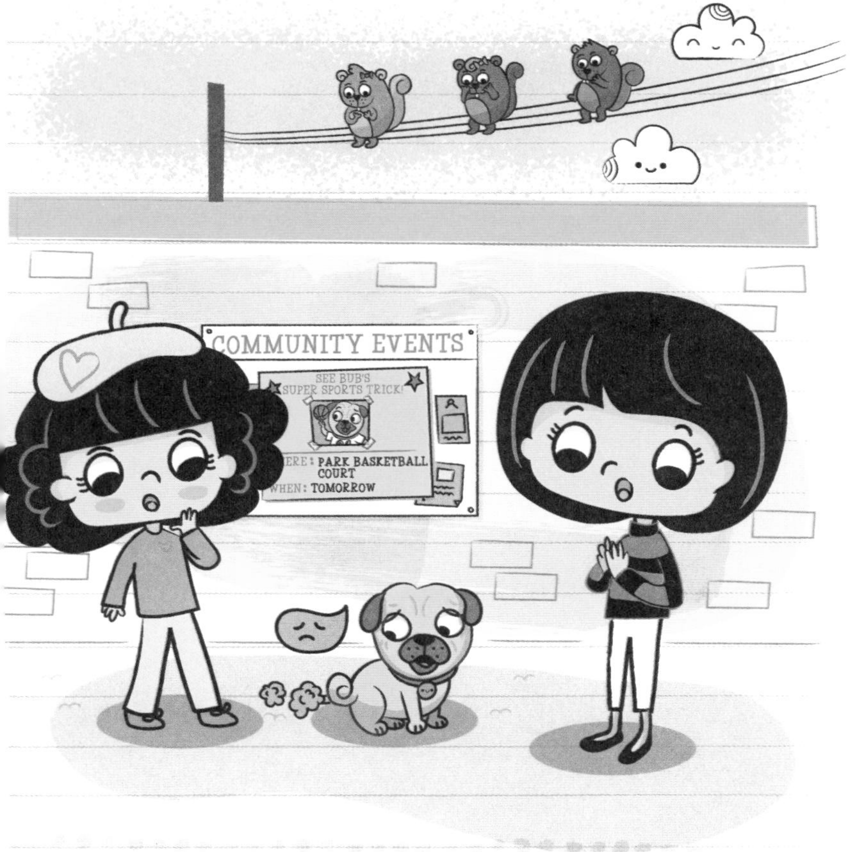
COMMUNITY EVENTS
SEE BUB'S SUPER SPORTS TRICK!
ERE: PARK BASKETBALL COURT
HEN: TOMORROW

But I didn't have time to worry because my squirrel fans were back!

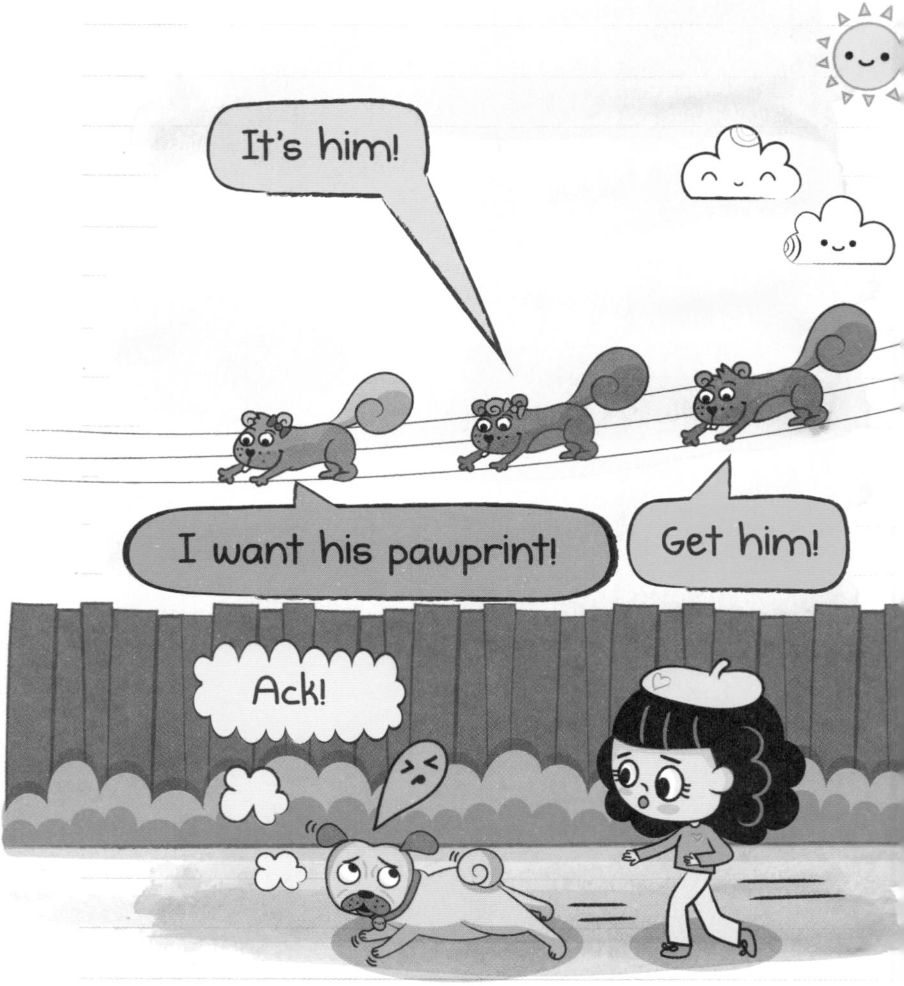
It's him!
I want his pawprint!
Get him!
Ack!

What am I going to do, Diary? Everyone thinks I'm a star. Especially Bella. What if I mess up in front of the whole town?

Chapter 6

MISSING THE HOOP

SATURDAY

Today was the big day, Diary. Bella walked me to the park basketball court.

SEE BUB'S
SUPER SPORTS TRICK!

WHERE: PARK BASKETBALL COURT
WHEN: TOMORROW

Everyone in town was there. They were cheering my name. Kids even wanted my pawprint autograph.

Diary, I was famous. And I felt more nervous than ever!

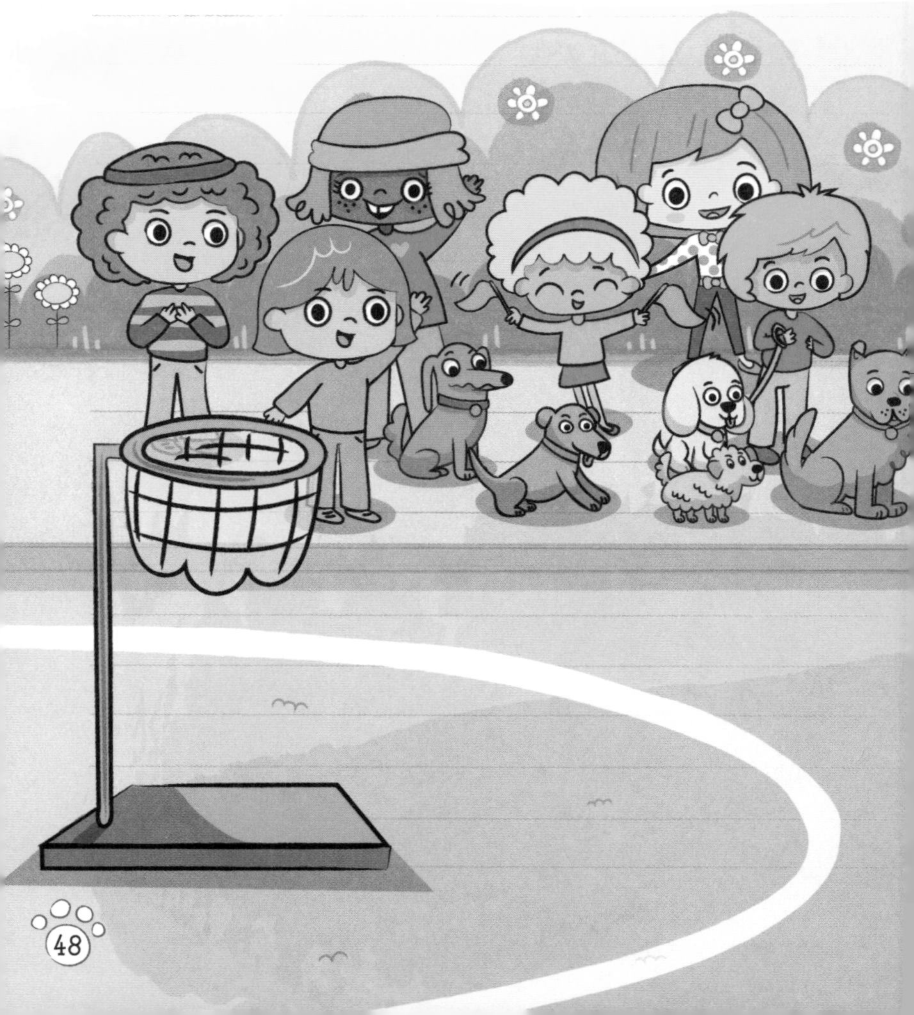

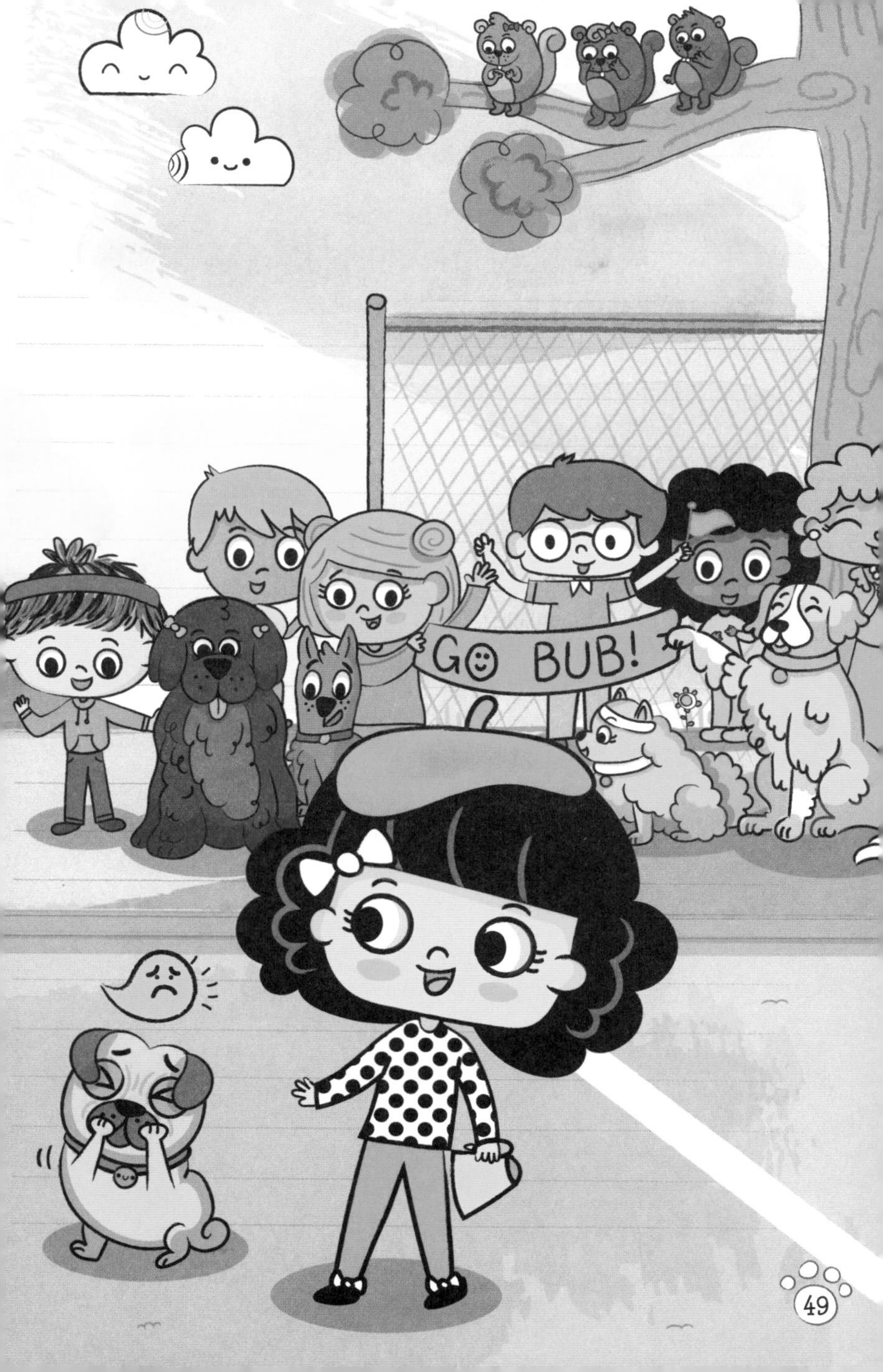
GO BUB!

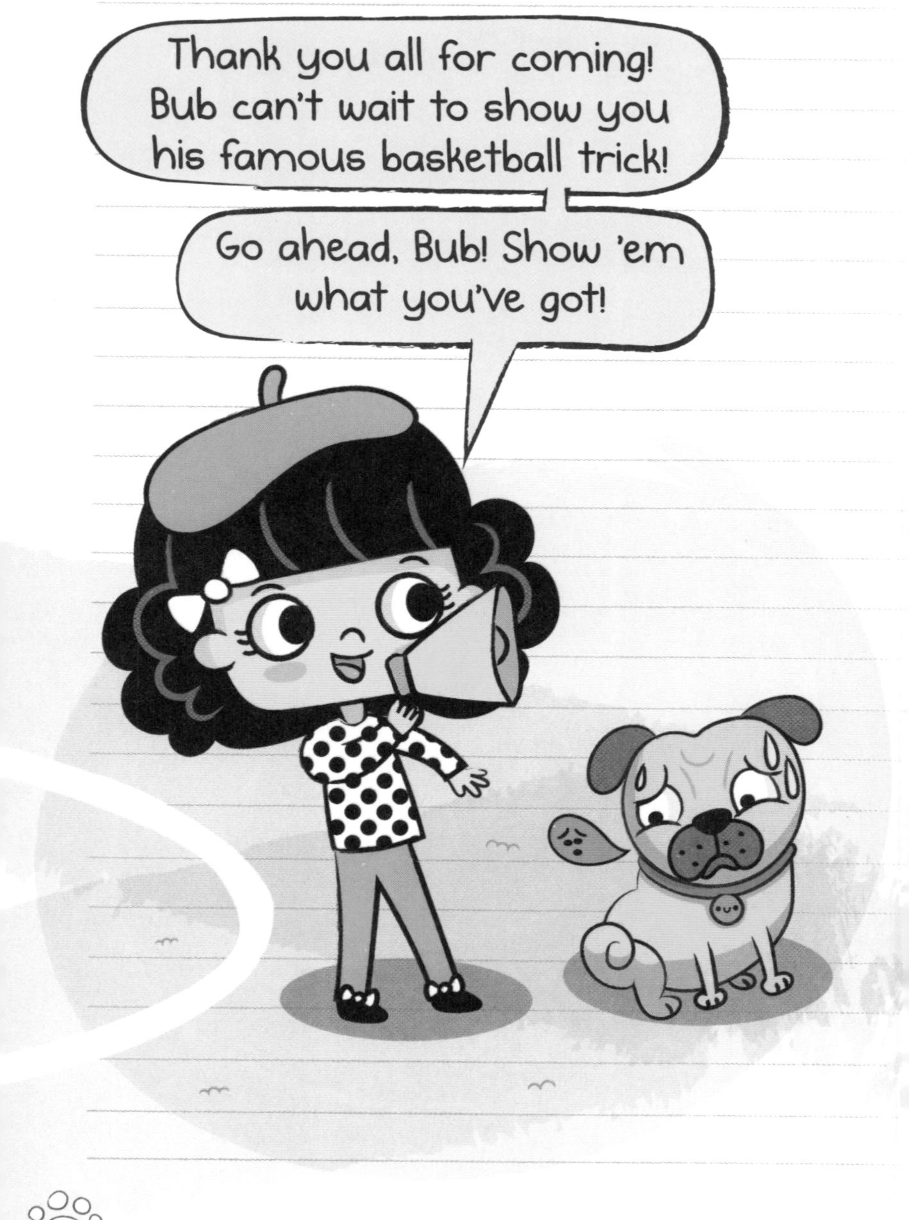
Thank you all for coming! Bub can't wait to show you his famous basketball trick!
Go ahead, Bub! Show 'em what you've got!

But it didn't go as planned, Diary.

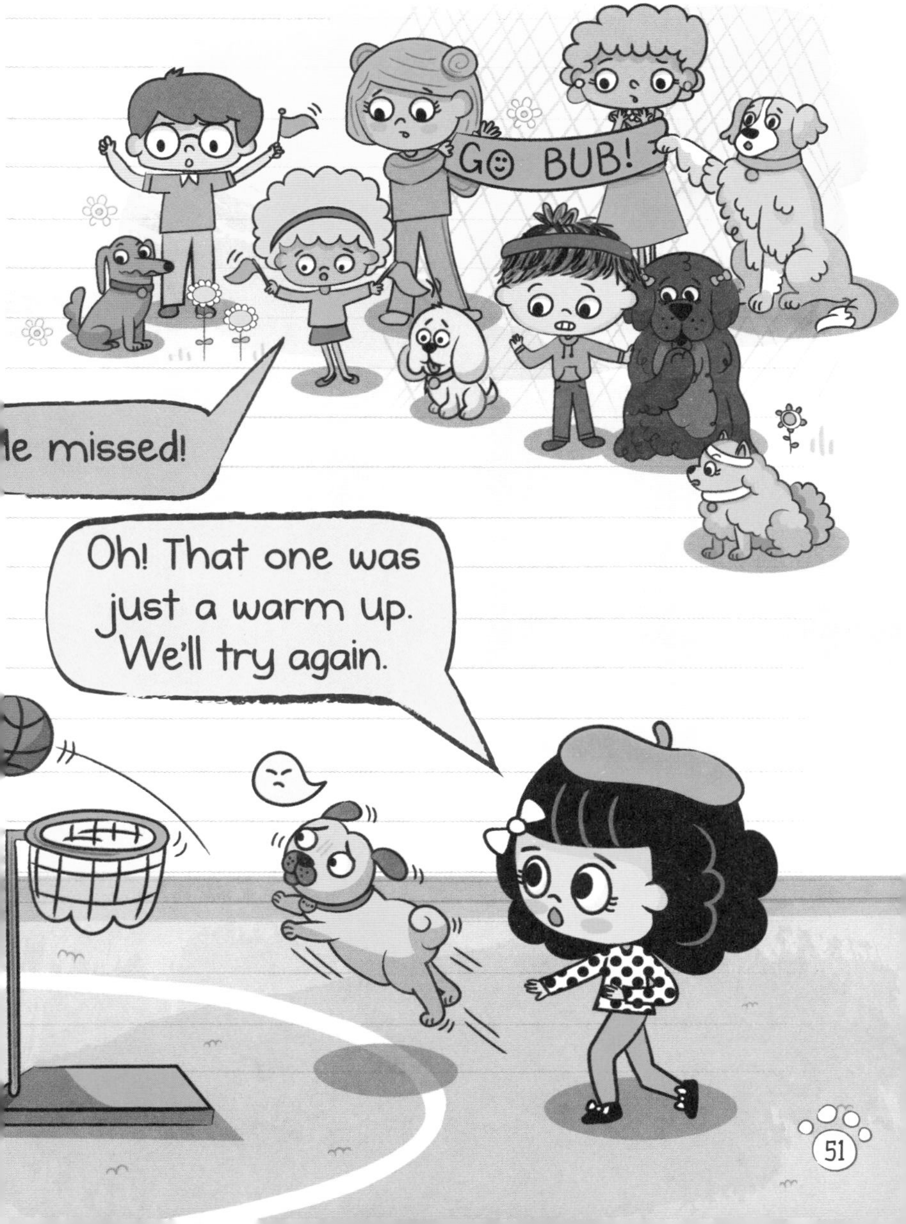
GO BUB!
le missed!
Oh! That one was just a warm up. We'll try again.

It was my worst nightmare, Diary. I tried shot after shot after shot. But I kept missing the hoop.

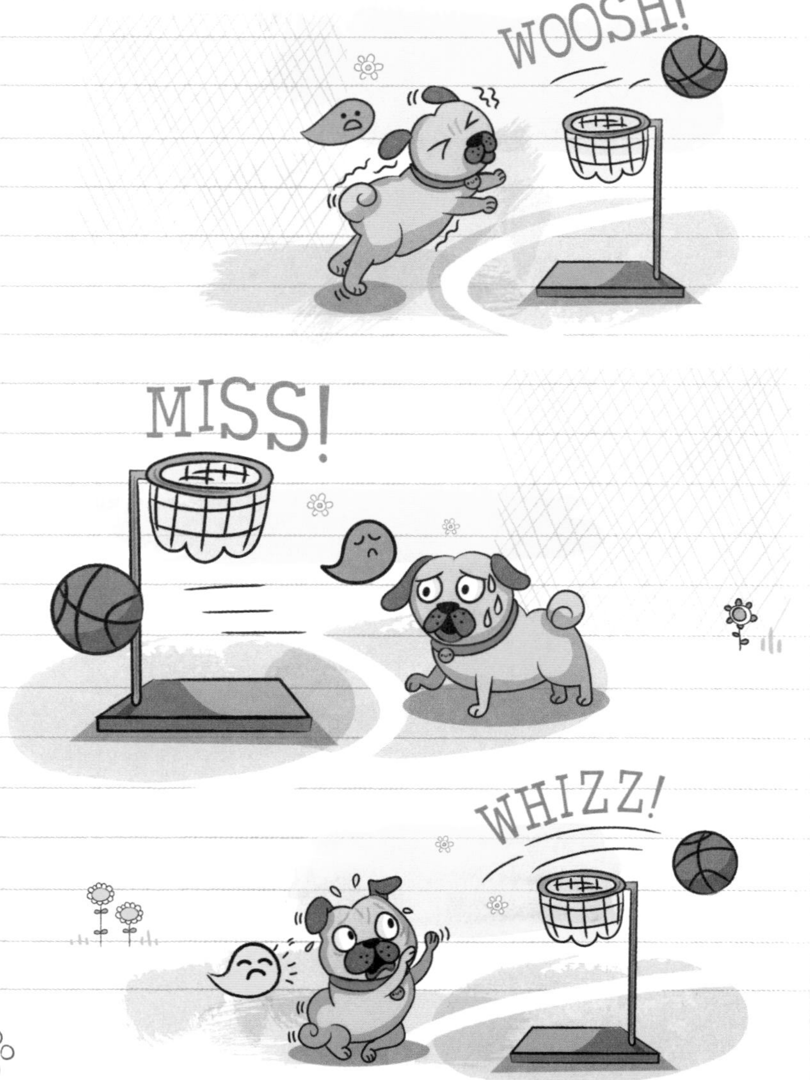
WOOSH!
MISS!
WHIZZ!

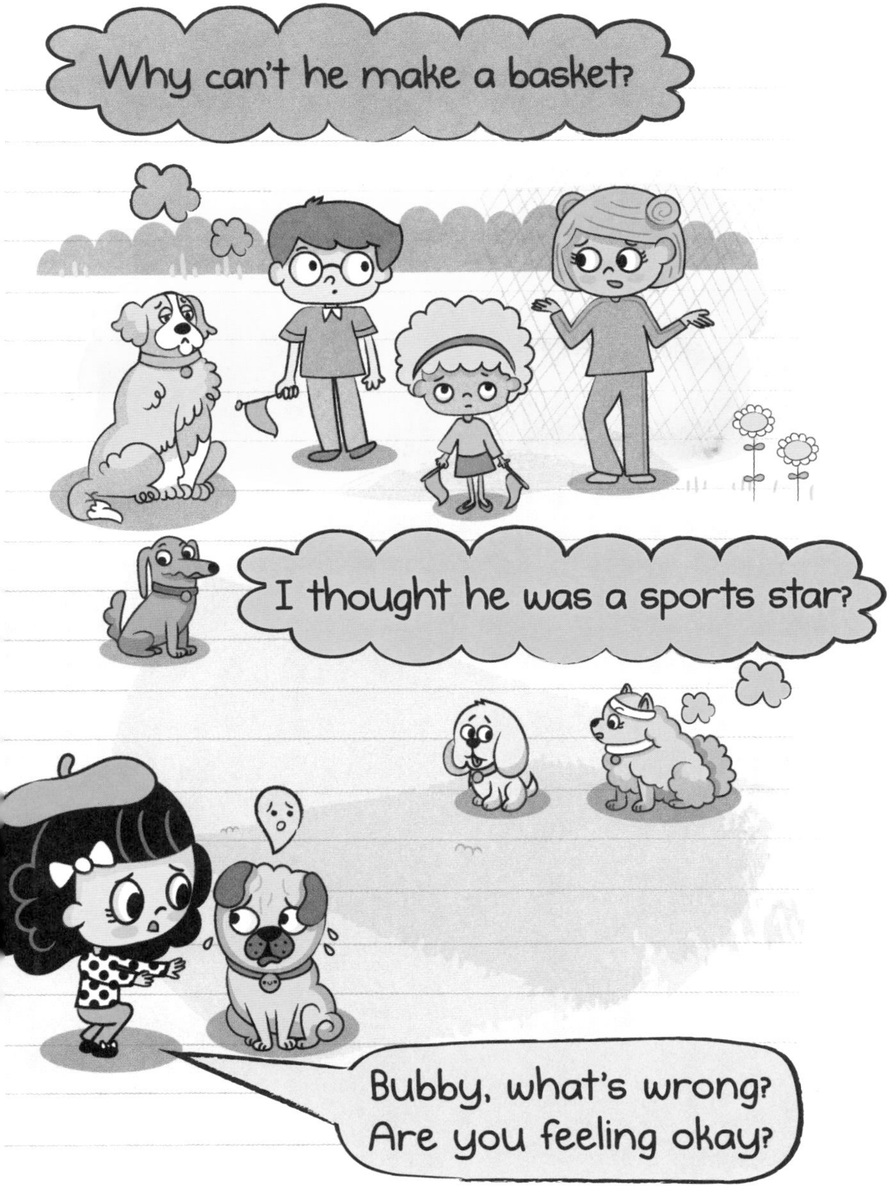
Why can't he make a basket?
I thought he was a sports star?
Bubby, what's wrong?
Are you feeling okay?

Then, the unthinkable happened . . .

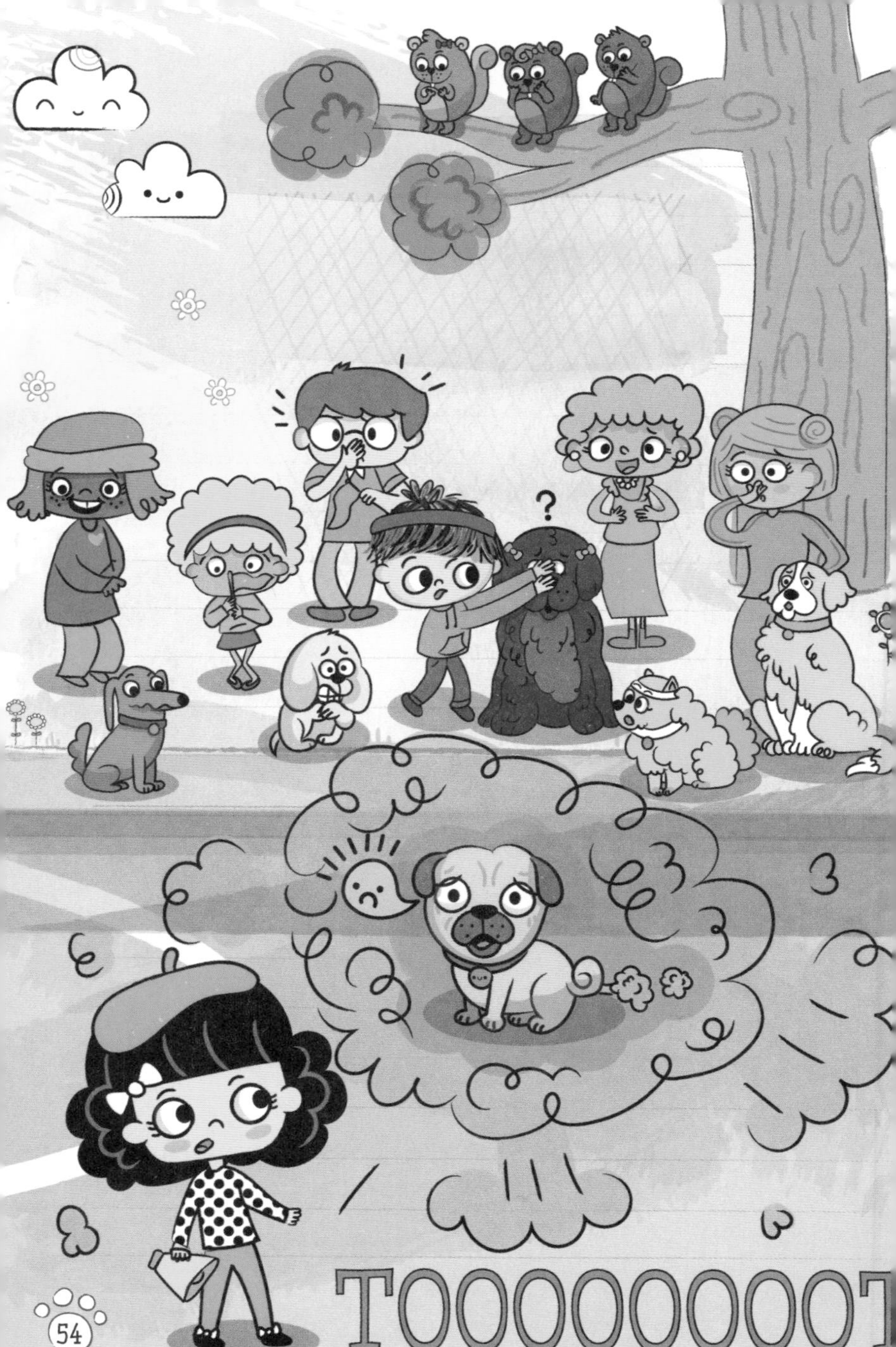
?
TOOOOOOOOT

I had tooted on the court — in front of the whole town! I had to get out of there!

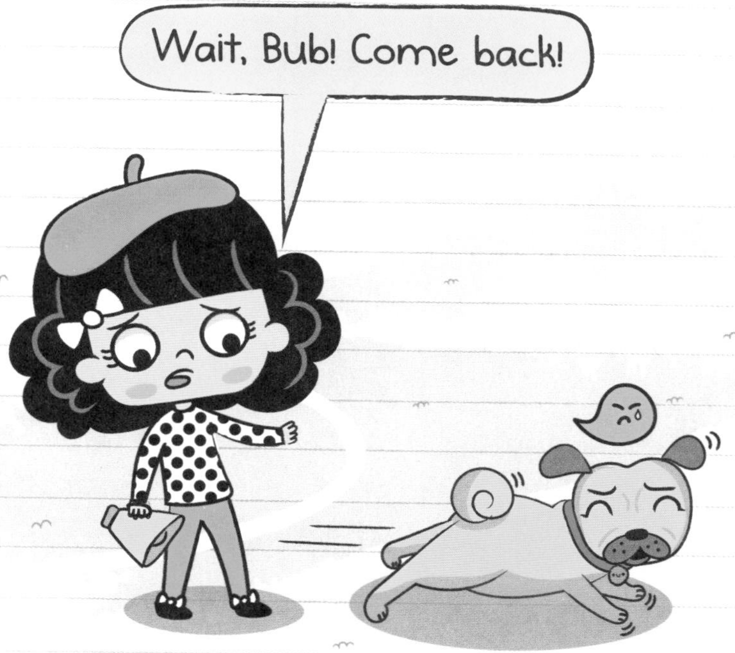
Wait, Bub! Come back!

Bella kept calling me, but I was too embarrassed to face her. I ran all the way home. My sports-star days were over!

Chapter 7

A HOOP–FUL IDEA

SUNDAY

Dear Diary,

I spent all day under my blanket. Bella tried to cheer me up with peanut butter pancakes. But I wasn't hungry.

Bubby, I'm so sorry. I put too much pressure on you.

No, I'm the one who messed up.

Jack and Luna came over and tried to cheer me up, too. But I was too ashamed to even say hi.

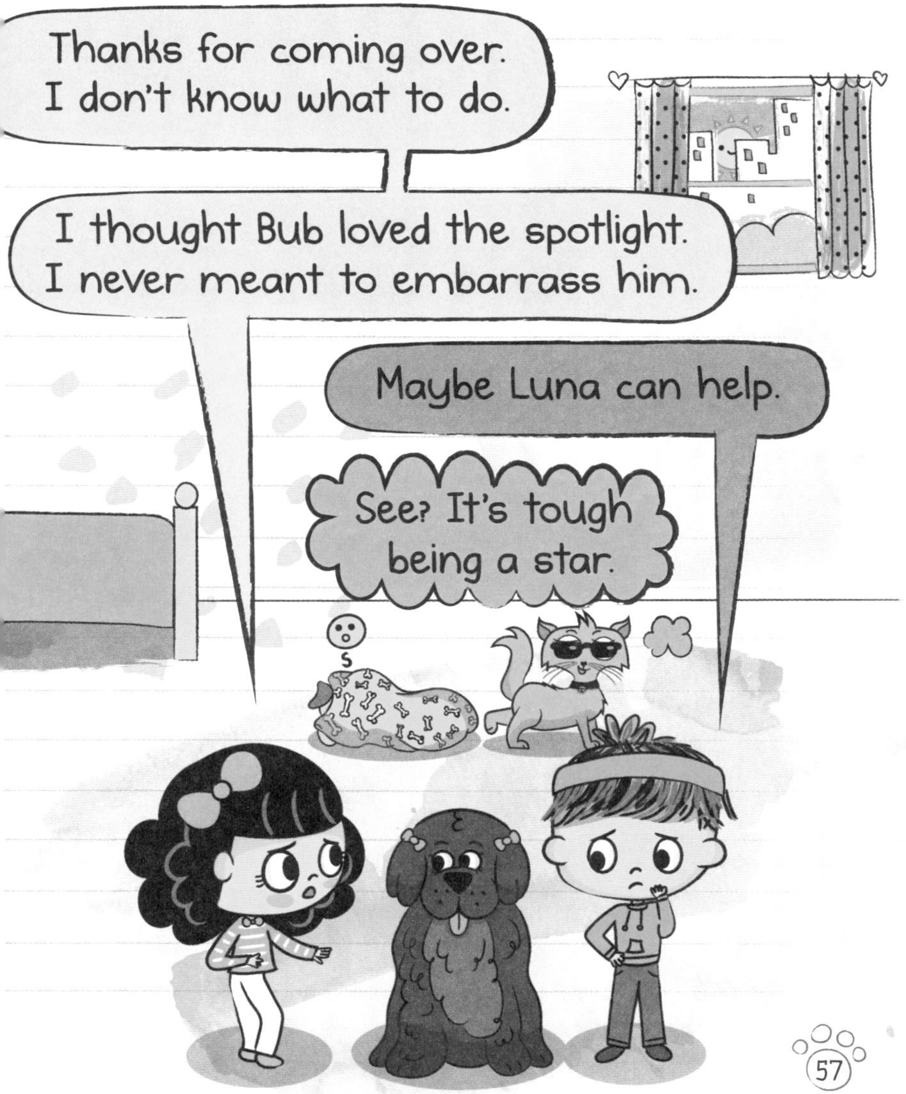
Thanks for coming over. I don't know what to do.
I thought Bub loved the spotlight. I never meant to embarrass him.
Maybe Luna can help.
See? It's tough being a star.

Luna tried to cheer me up.

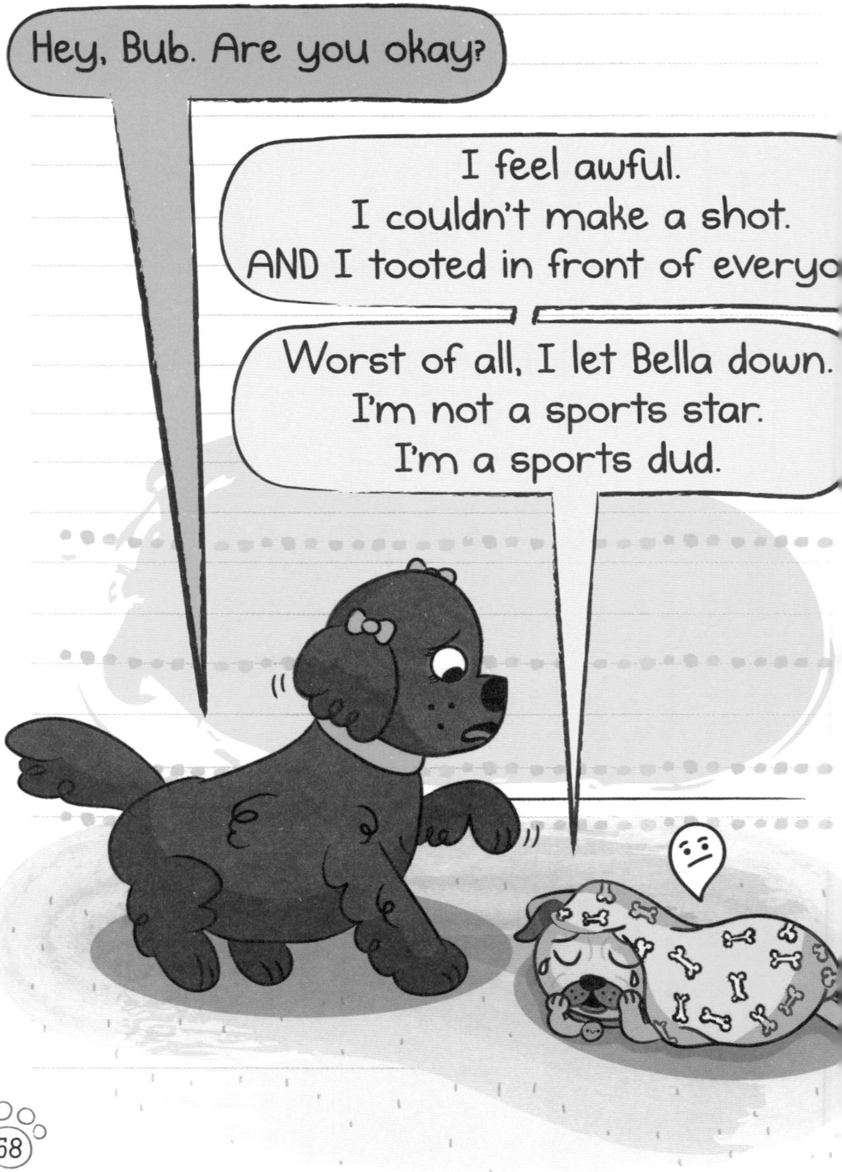

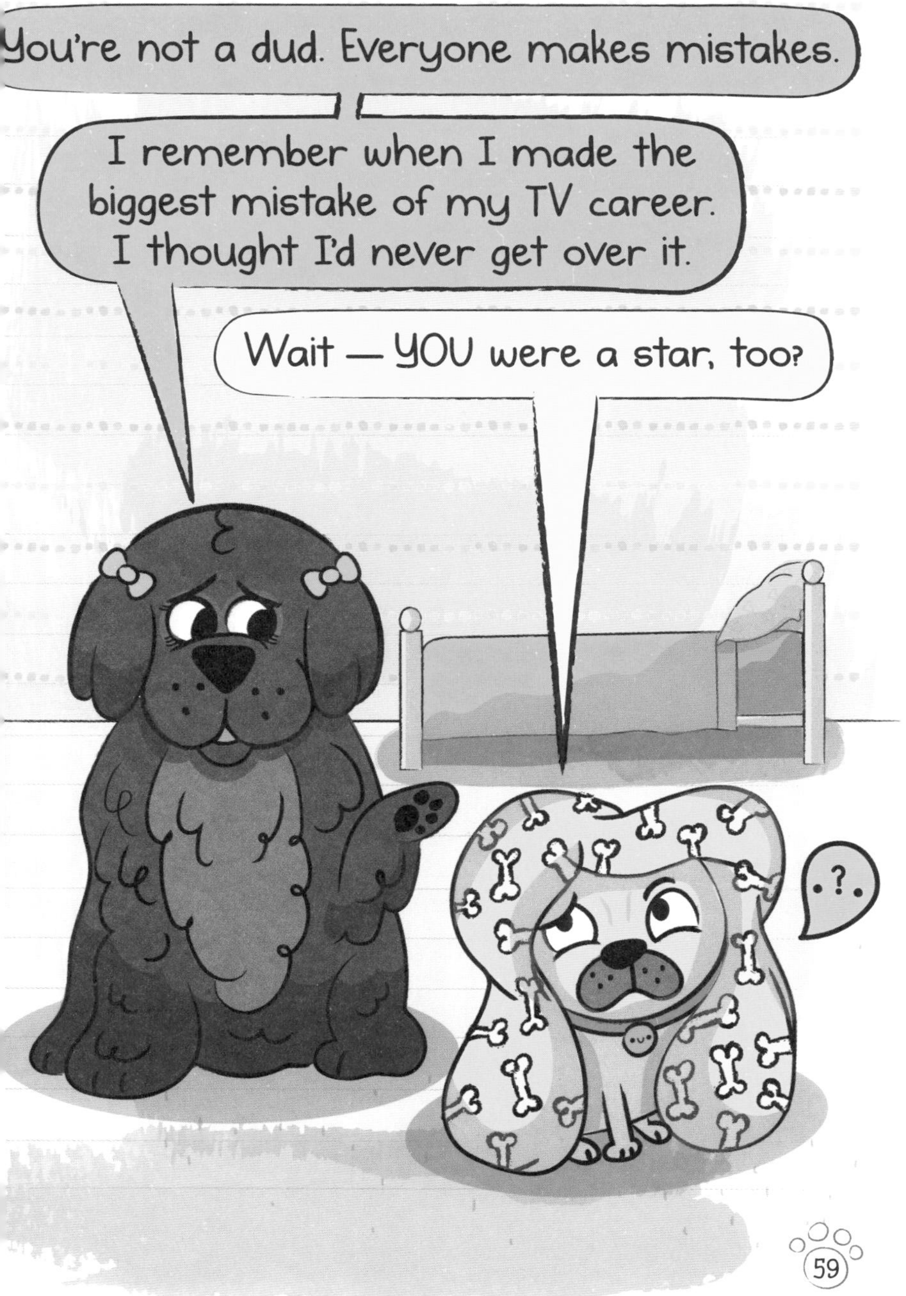
You're not a dud. Everyone makes mistakes.
I remember when I made the biggest mistake of my TV career. I thought I'd never get over it.
Wait — YOU were a star, too?
?

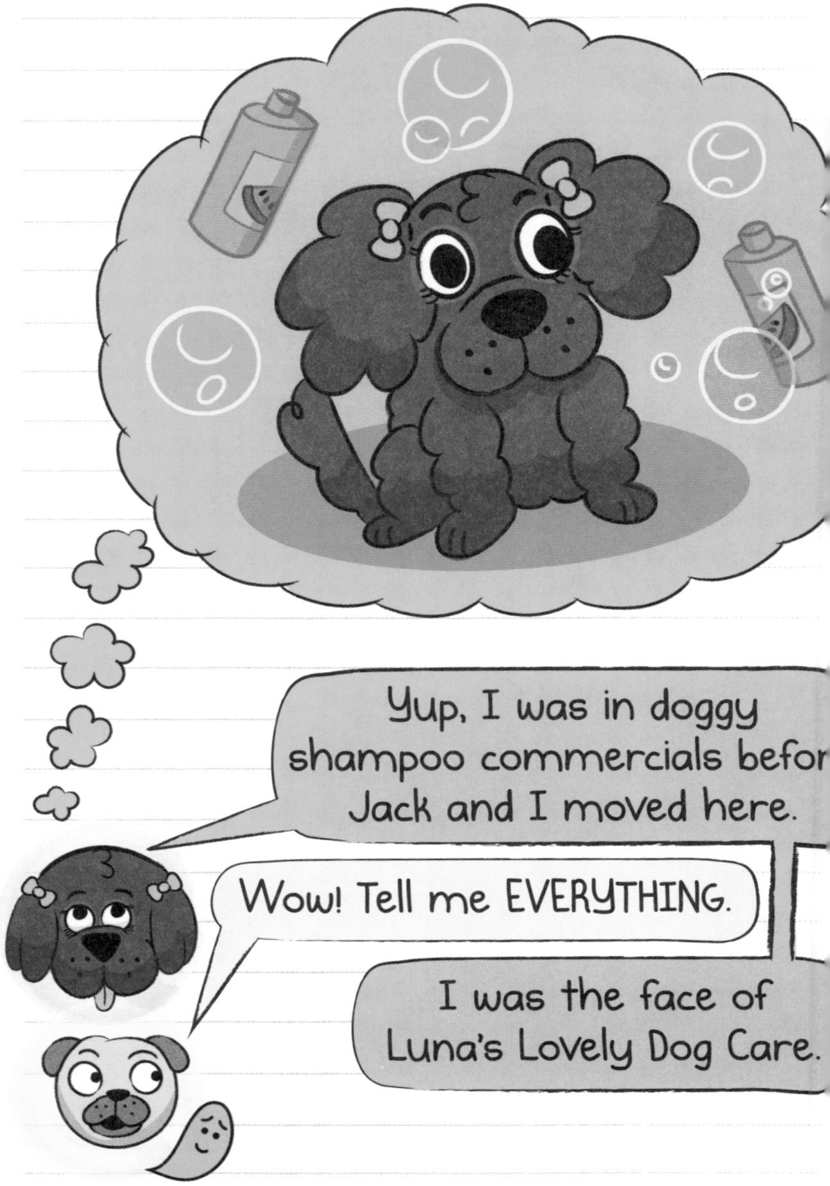
Yup, I was in doggy shampoo commercials befor
Jack and I moved here.
Wow! Tell me EVERYTHING.
I was the face of Luna's Lovely Dog Care.

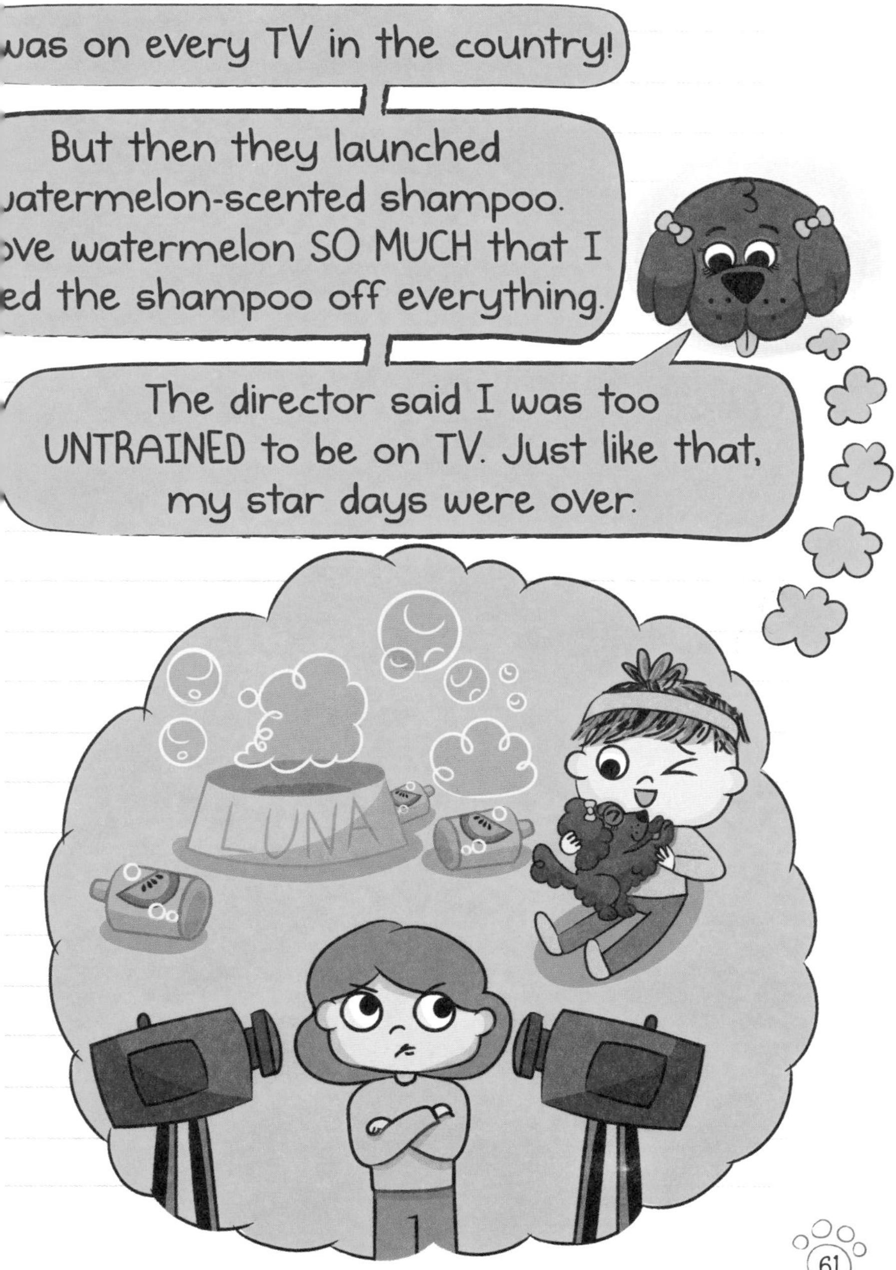
was on every TV in the country!
But then they launched
atermelon-scented shampoo.
ove watermelon SO MUCH that I
ed the shampoo off everything.
The director said I was too UNTRAINED to be on TV. Just like that, my star days were over.
LUNA

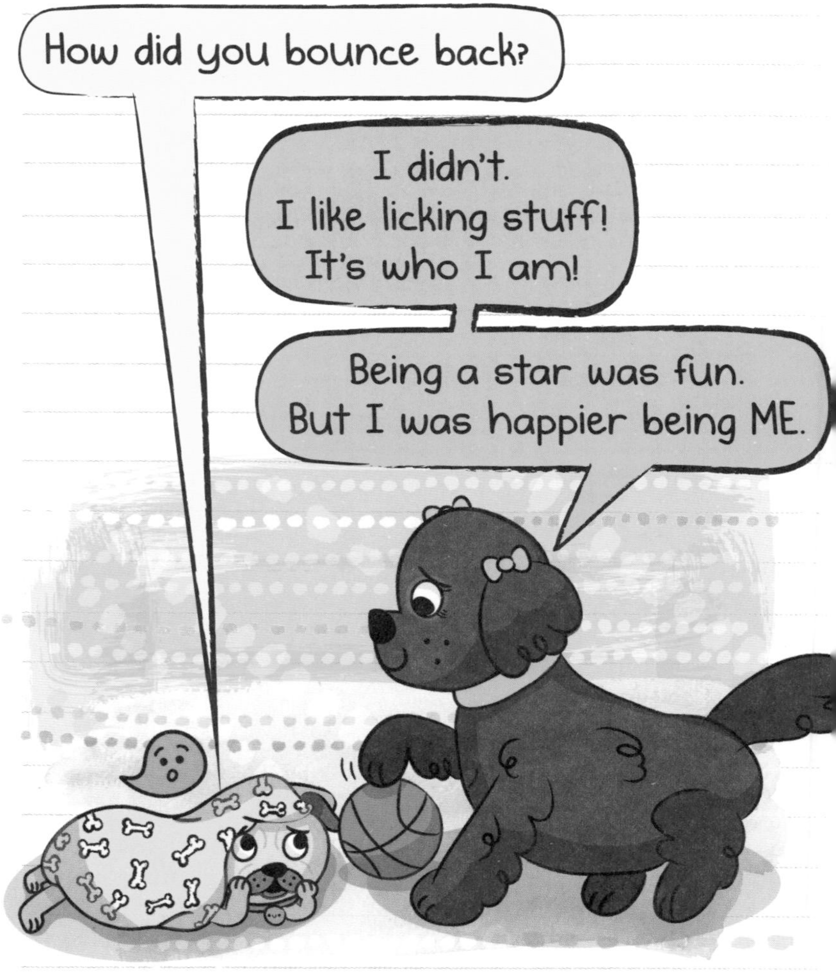
How did you bounce back?
I didn't.
I like licking stuff!
It's who I am!
Being a star was fun.
But I was happier being ME.

I thought about what Luna said.

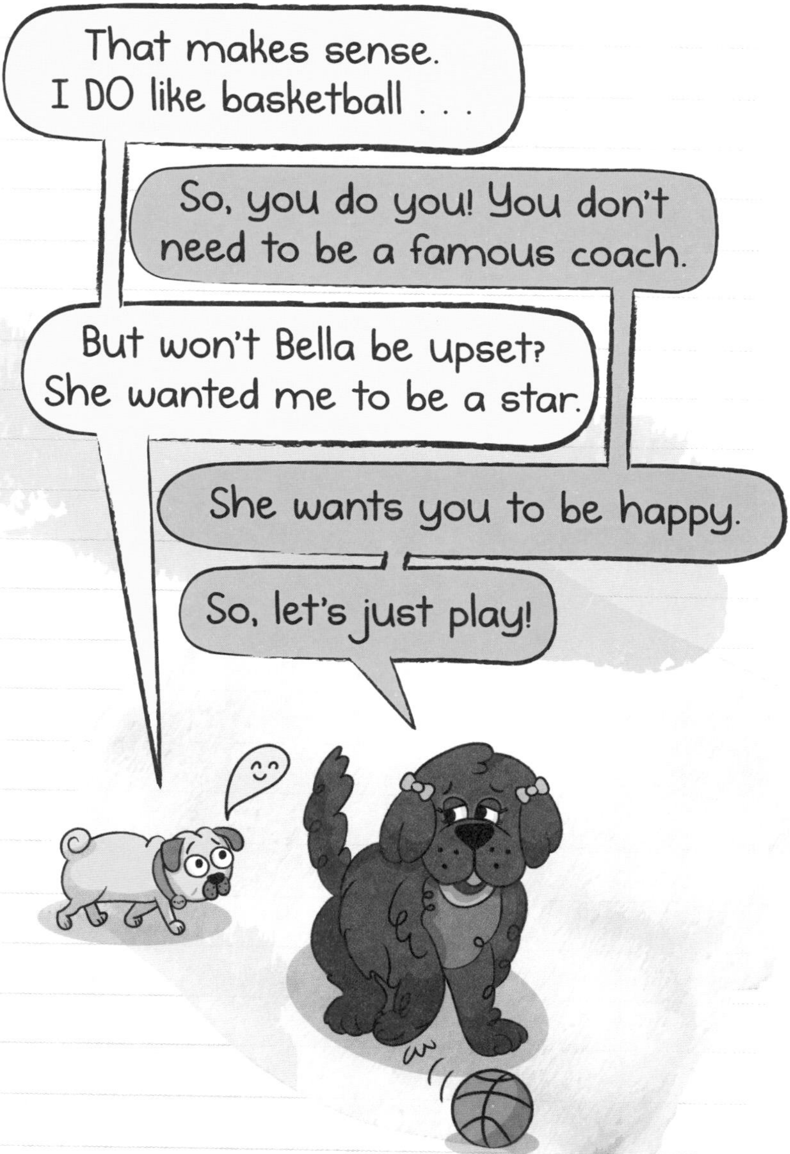
That makes sense.
I DO like basketball . . .
So, you do you! You don't need to be a famous coach.
But won't Bella be upset? She wanted me to be a star.
She wants you to be happy.
So, let's just play!

I followed Luna outside.

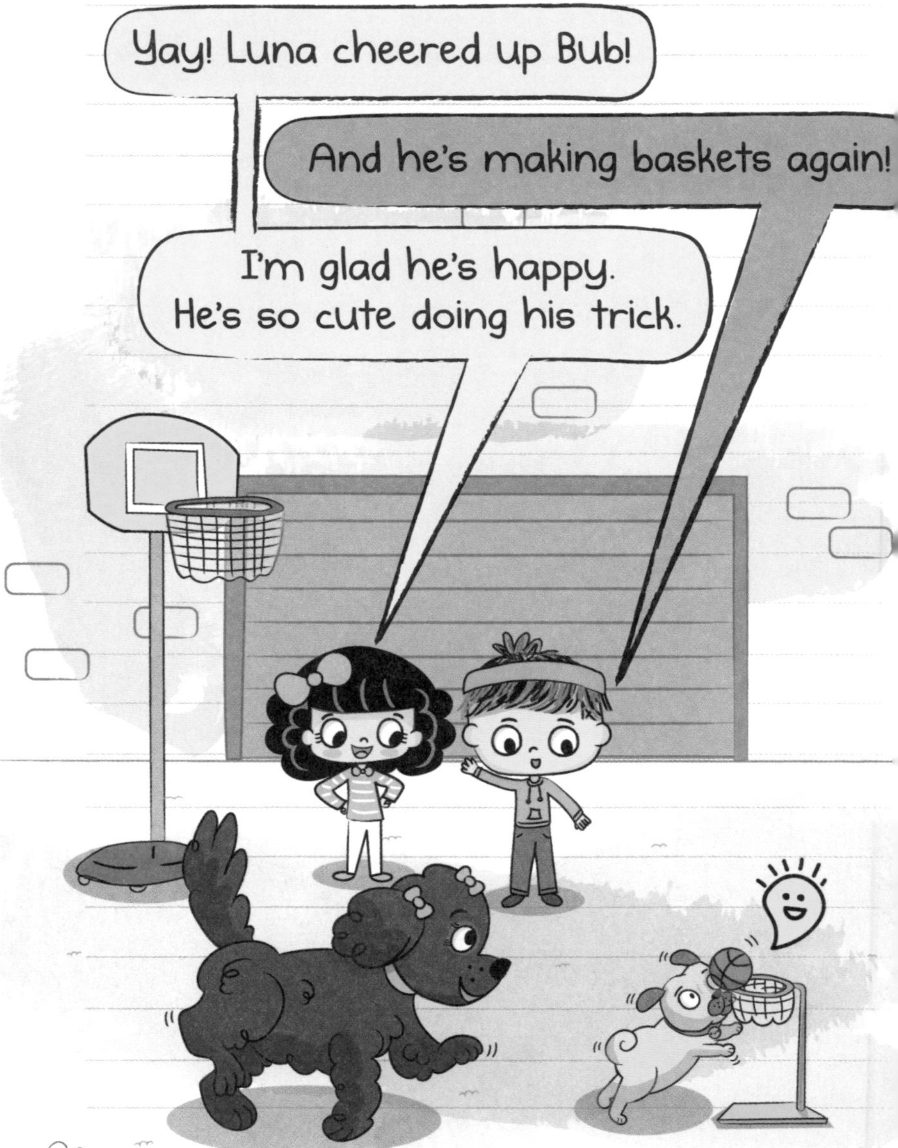
Yay! Luna cheered up Bub!
And he's making baskets again!
I'm glad he's happy.
He's so cute doing his trick.

Diary, watching me gave Bella a new idea.

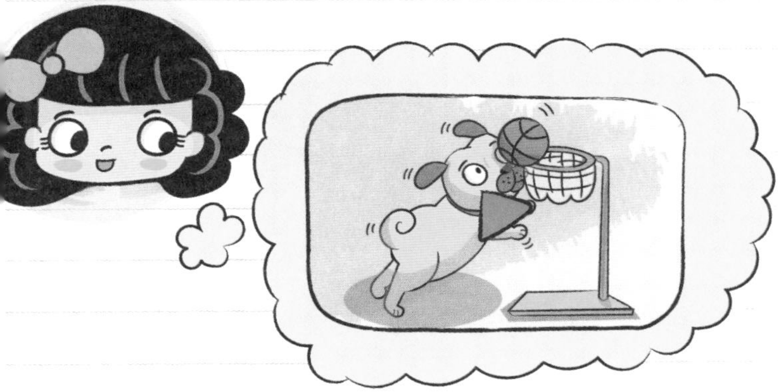

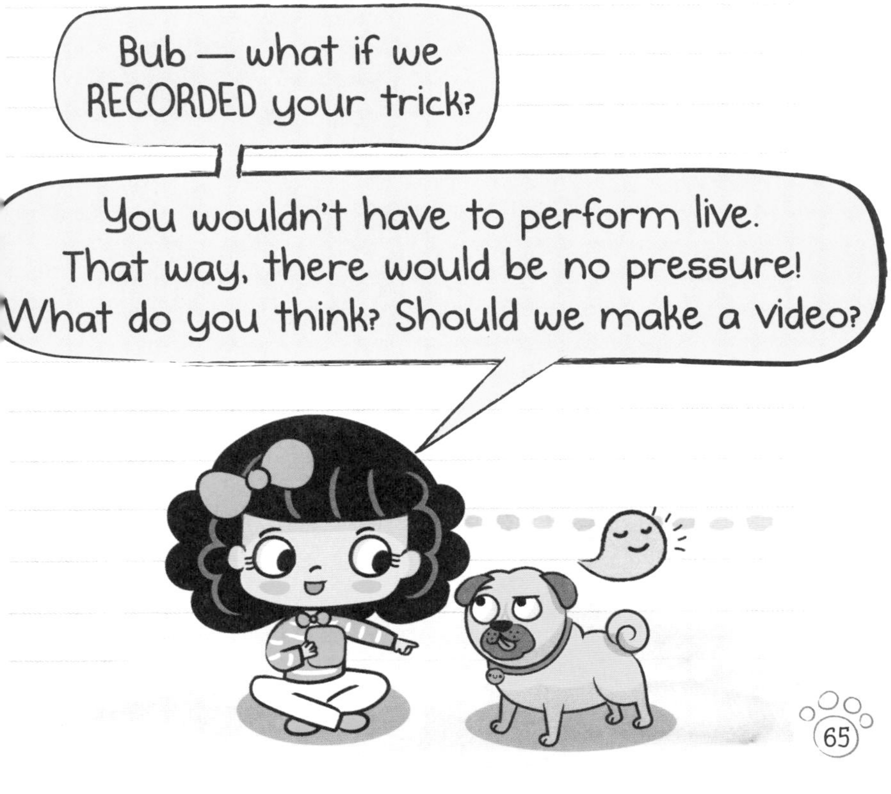
Bub — what if we RECORDED your trick?
You wouldn't have to perform live. That way, there would be no pressure! What do you think? Should we make a video?

I LOVED Bella's idea, Diary! I could still show off my cool moves, but I didn't have to do it over and over again or get nervous in front of a big crowd.

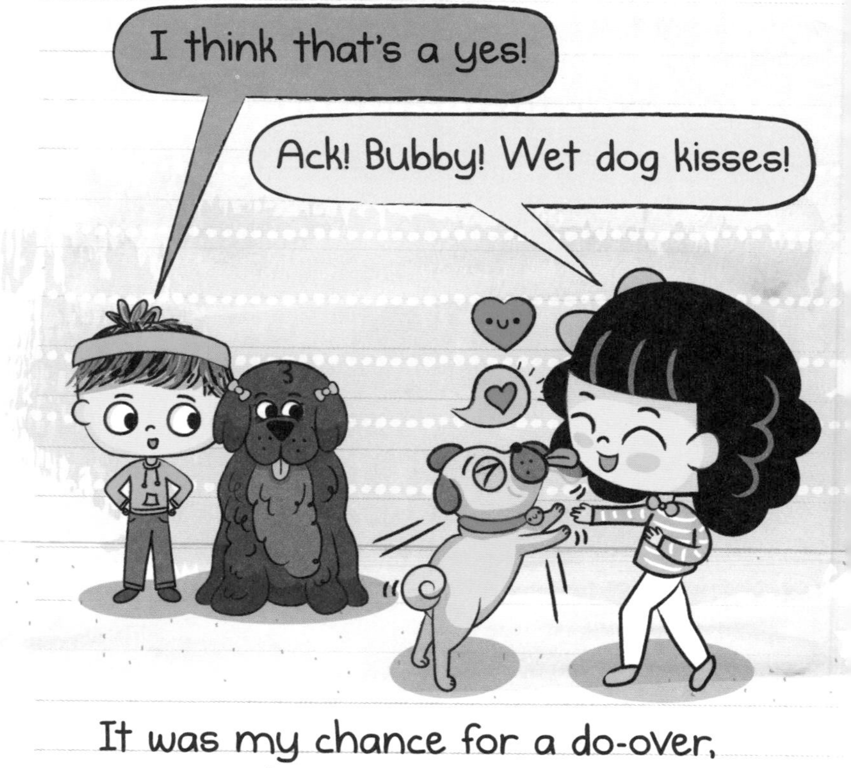
I think that's a yes!
Ack! Bubby! Wet dog kisses!

It was my chance for a do-over, Diary. But this time, I would be playing for ME! Who knows? Maybe Bub the sports star was back!

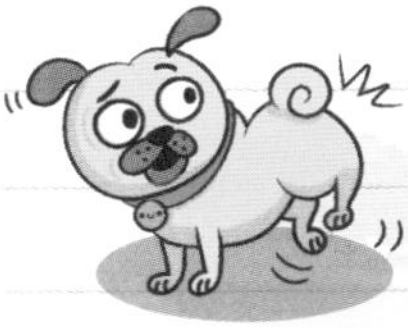

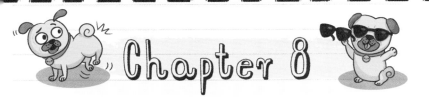

Chapter 8

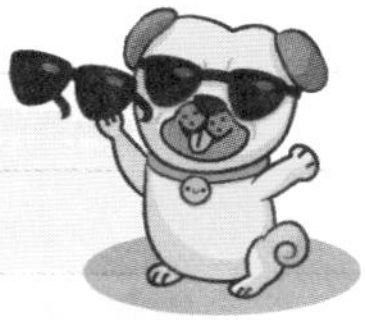

ONE LAST HOOP

MONDAY

Dear Diary,

Bella invited everyone to our backyard after school today. I helped her set up the big reveal.

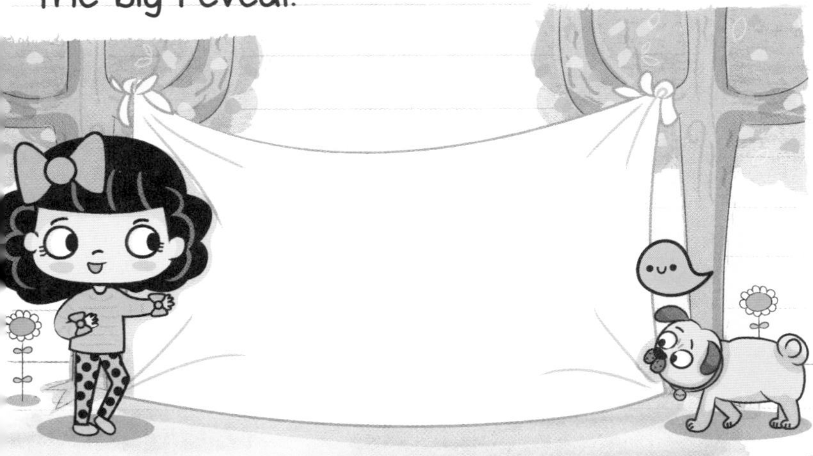

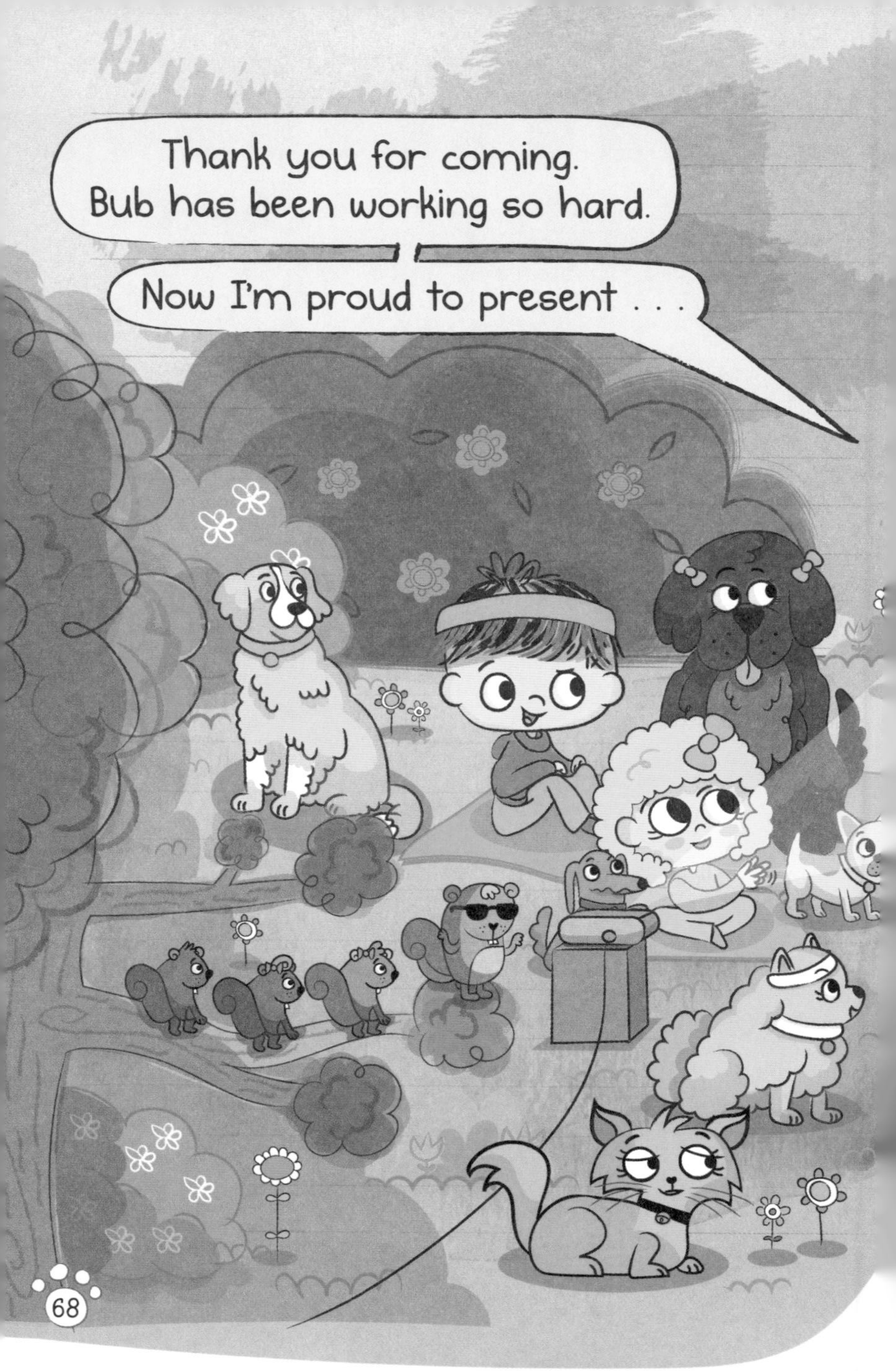
Thank you for coming. Bub has been working so hard.
Now I'm proud to present . . .

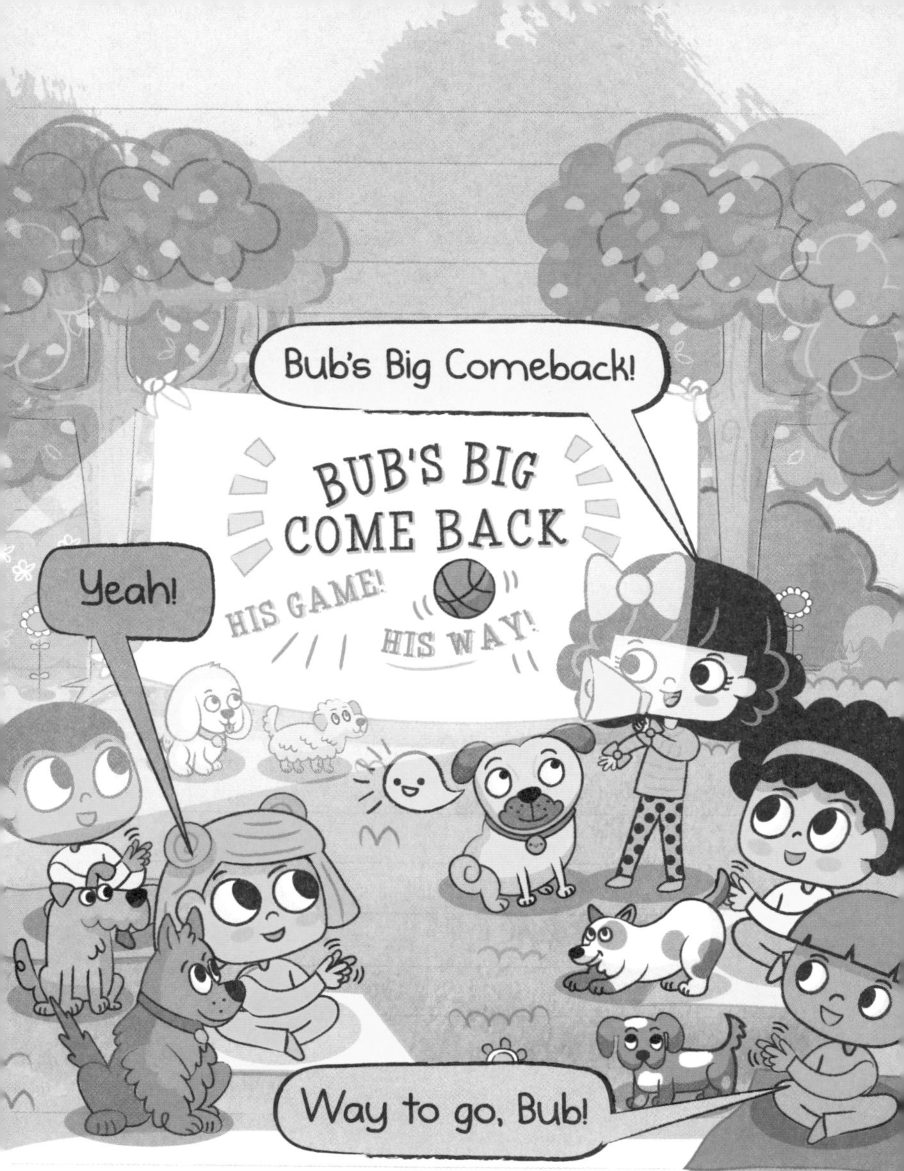
Bub's Big Comeback!
BUB'S BIG
COME BACK
HIS GAME!
HIS WAY!
Yeah!
Way to go, Bub!

The audience watched the video, Diary! And guess what?

They LOVED it! They especially liked the new and improved tricks I'd thrown in. Bella had told me to just have fun. So, that's what I did!

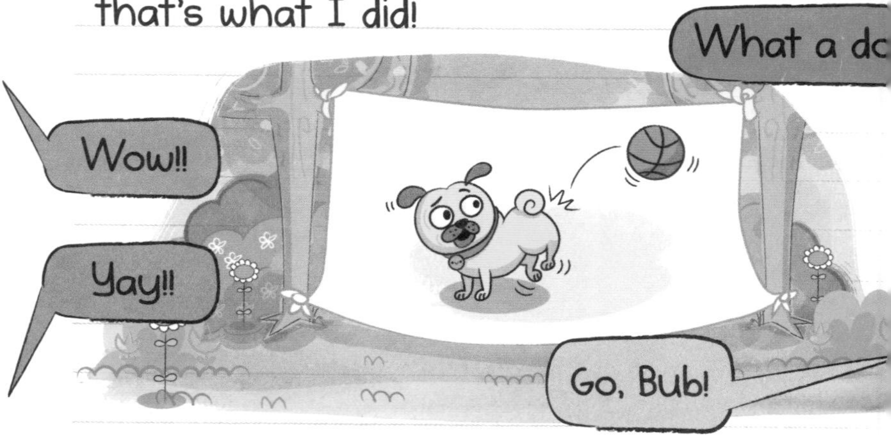
Wow!!
Yay!!
Go, Bub!

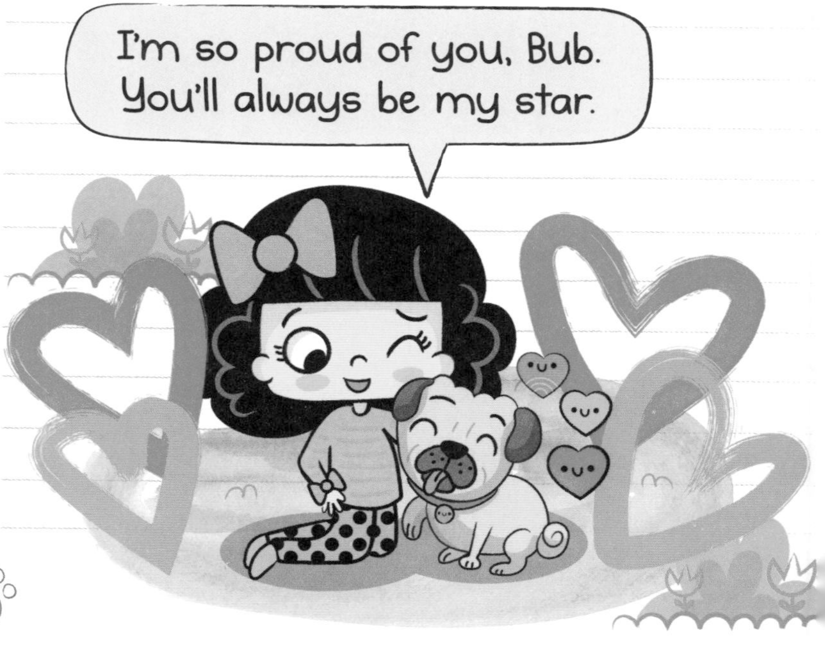
I'm so proud of you, Bub.
You'll always be my star.

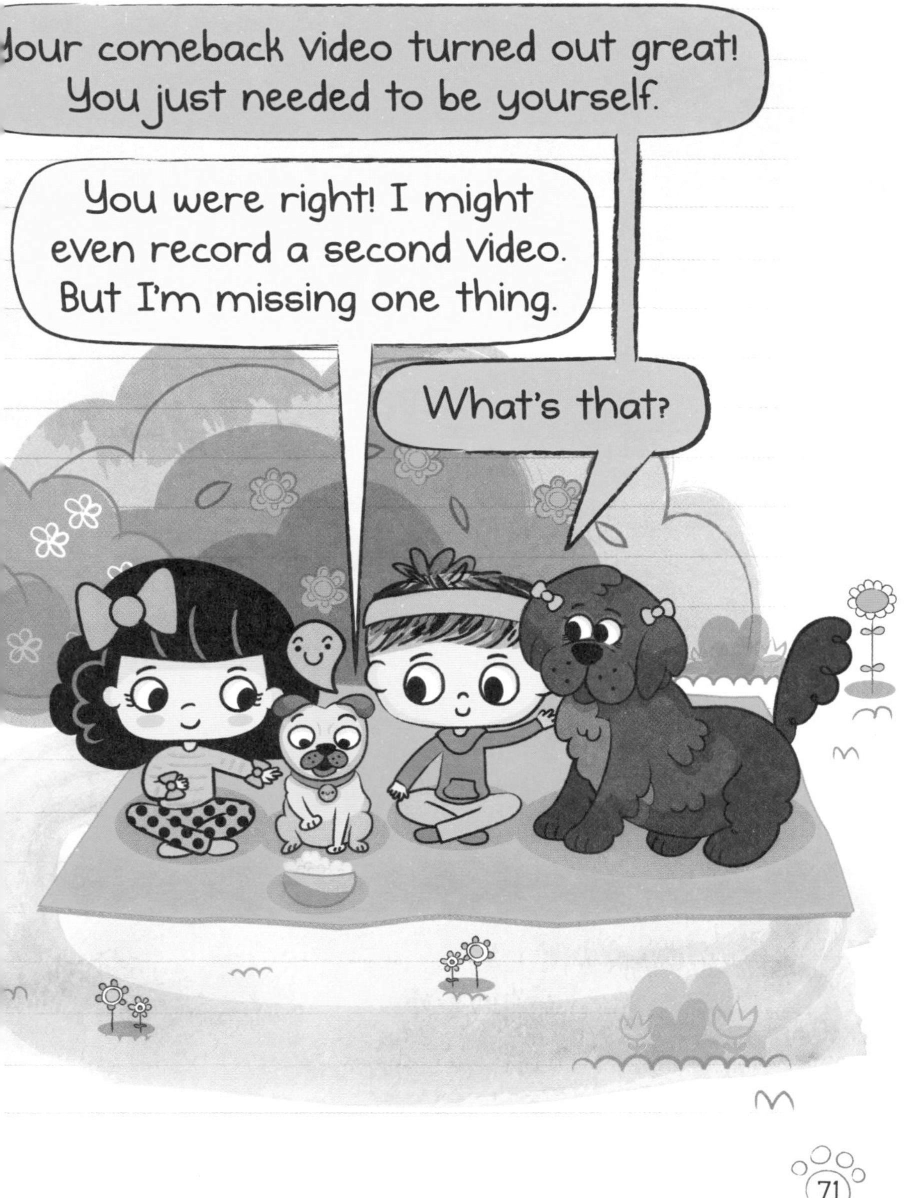
You comeback video turned out great! You just needed to be yourself.
You were right! I might even record a second video. But I'm missing one thing.
What's that?

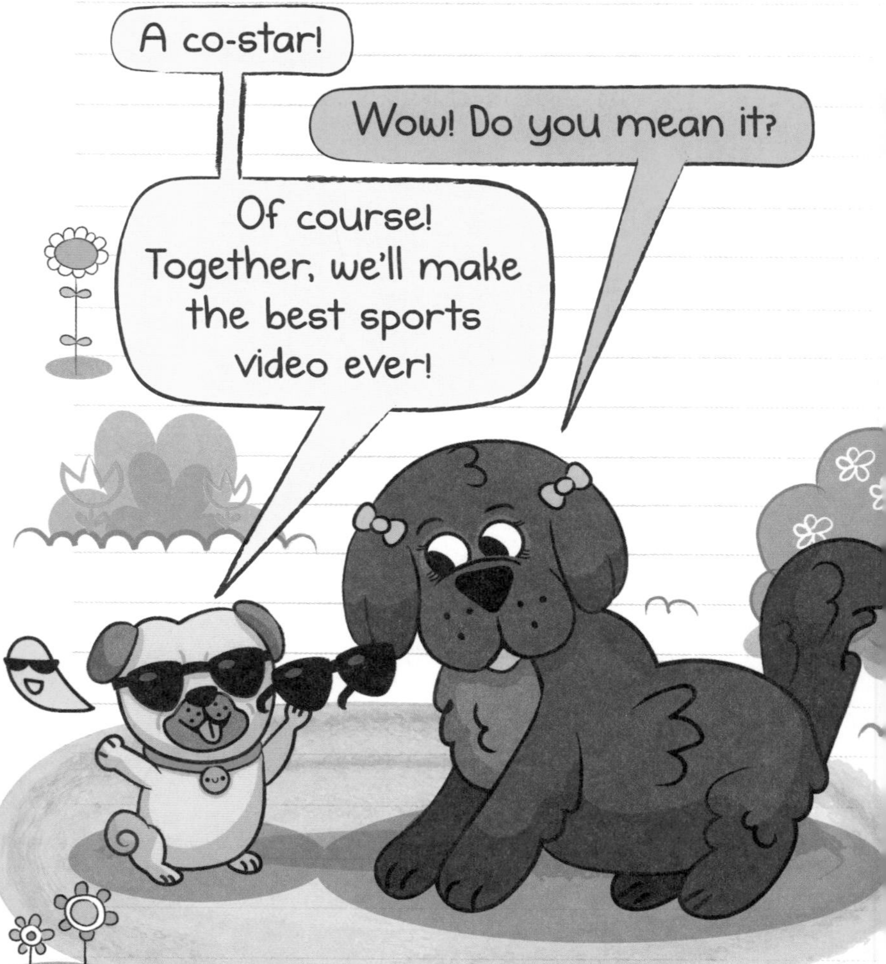
A co-star!
Wow! Do you mean it?
Of course! Together, we'll make the best sports video ever!

Being a star is fun, Diary! But you know what else is fun? Just being me!

About the Creator

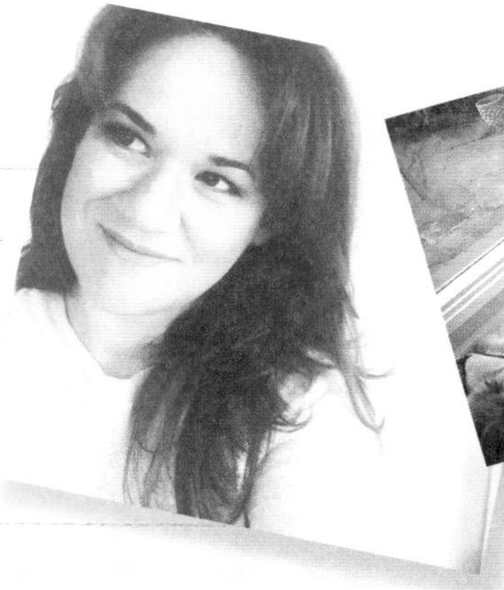

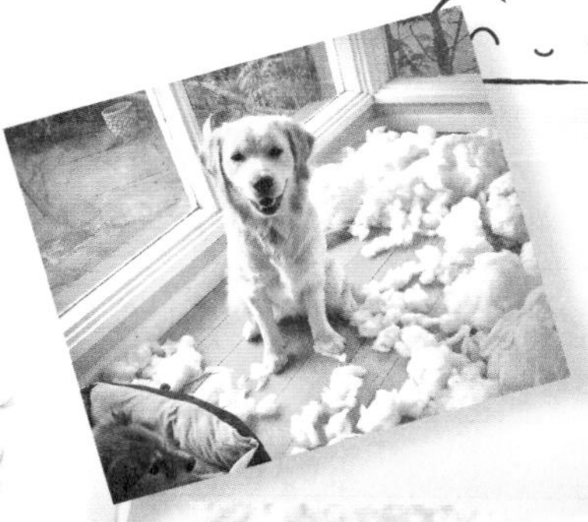

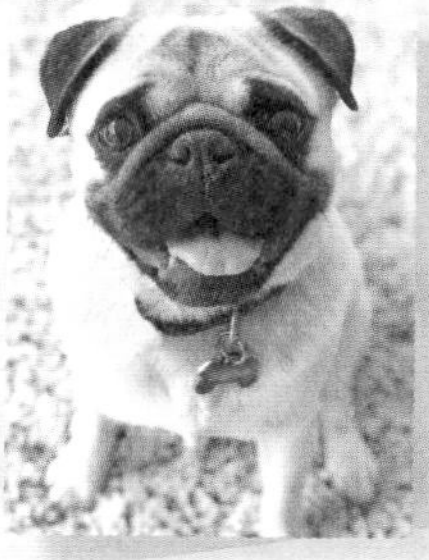

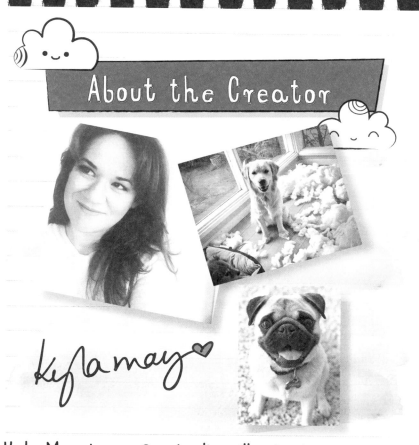

Kyla May

Kyla May is an Australian illustrator, writer, and designer. In addition to books, Kyla creates animation. She lives by the beach in Victoria, Australia, with her three daughters, two cats, and two dogs. Bub the Pug was inspired by her daughter's pug.

HOW MUCH DO YOU KNOW ABOUT

DIARY OF A PUG

Pug the Sports Star?

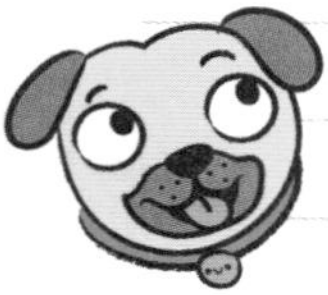

What makes me interested in learning to play basketball?

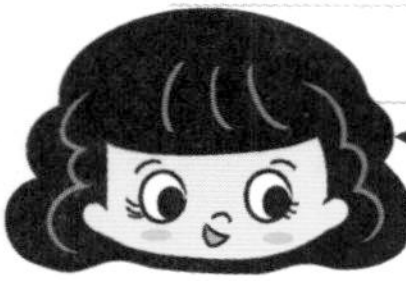

What do I make Bub in my art class so he'll look like a real sports star?

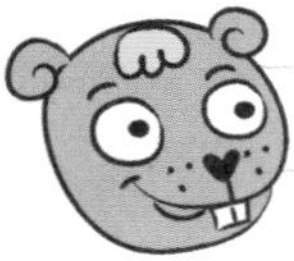

What is an autograph? Reread pages 20 and 38 – 39 if you need help figuring it out! Have you ever gotten someone's autograph?

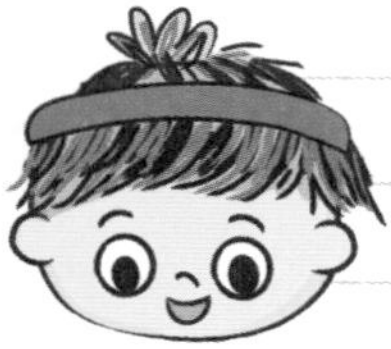

If you could teach a dog a new trick, what would it be?

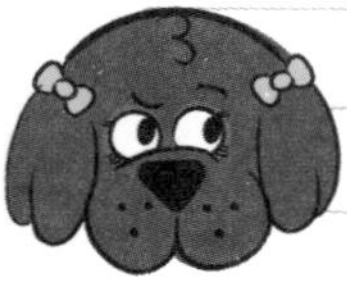

What advice do I give Bub about being a star?

scholastic.com/branches